ANCIENT WAYS

Book Fifteen of the Hayle Coven Novels

I0556103

PATTI LARSEN

ALSO BY
PATTI LARSEN

The Hayle Coven Universe

The Hunted Series
Fiona Fleming Cozy Mysteries
The Nightshade Cases
The Clone Chronicles
The Diamond City Trilogy
Didi and the Gunslinger

and much, much more.
Find your new favorite author at
pattilarsen.com
Sign up for new releases
bit.ly/pattilarsenemail

CHAPTER ONE

Sweat stung my eyes, the thud of my hands against the heavy bag vibrating up my arms and into my chest. I leaned back and lashed out with one foot in a roundhouse, connecting solidly with the cracked vinyl, the chain creaking as I sent the bag swinging.

"Nice hit." I turned, wiping my face on the shoulder of my t-shirt to the grinning face of my kick-boxing instructor. Sage steadied the bag, deep green eyes smiling as much as his mouth.

A rather yummy mouth, as it turned out. Nice little chin-cleft, too, a bit of beard shadow roughing up his wide jaw, dark brows framing that sea-colored gaze. Thick lashes framed his eyes, lashes I was jealous of the moment I walked into the gym and he looked up to greet me.

With that same smile he gave me now.

"I'm feeling more balanced." I drew a deep breath, bobbed up and down on my toes as I faced off with the bag again. "That tip you gave me about staying lower really helped."

He shrugged, his tanned skin rippling under his black tank with "Arno's Gym" straining across the front over his very nicely developed pecs. "Anything I can do to help," he said in his tenor voice. Mellow, soft for such a big guy. Sage stood almost as tall as Liam, though he had more of Quaid's bulk.

Yup, comparing boys. Fun stuff.

The only difference, this boy was normal. Completely. Not a trace of latent power to be felt. As Sage steadied the bag for me, one big shoulder holding it firm, his large hands gripping the sides for leverage, I found myself grinning.

Nothing wrong with normal now and then.

I felt my mood shift as my mind went to Liam and my decision to choose him, to see what we could do about the relationship he claimed he desperately wanted. Two thuds with my gloved fists released some of my returning tension.

Guess he didn't want to be with me as much as he said. If he did, we wouldn't have spent the last eight months with the elephant in the room that was his mother firmly placed between us, her false smile and need to be part of every single thing her son did driving me to contemplate murder.

Thud. Thud.

It felt good to let my anger out in a way that made me stronger instead of driving me to dismember and dispose of someone. Someone with salon perfect hair and the most grasping sense of ownership on the boy she'd given birth to and then served up to her Unseelie lordling master I'd ever had the misfortune to encounter.

Bitter, me? Naw.

Thud. Thud. Whack.

I caught a glimpse of Charlotte watching, standing in the corner with her arms crossed over her chest, glaring at Sage. All pissed off and wolf fur ruffled I'd decided to learn to fight.

When I told her my plans to find a gym when we came home to Wilding Springs a few weeks ago, she frowned.

"Why?" That was Charlotte. My bodywere was nothing if not blunt and to the point.

"I want to learn to defend myself," I said. She should be all for it, shouldn't she? Less worry for her. And for me.

Instead, she grunted. "That's what you have me for," she said, sounding hurt.

Seriously?

Ever since my little jaunt to the Sidhe realm, when I'd been forced to allow Shaylee and my demon to fight for me against the thralled Quaid, I'd realized just how vulnerable I was when I didn't have access to magic. Yes, I could run. So what? Anyone could do that. But, there were times when running wouldn't be an option.

Had happened now more times than I could count. Learning to fight instead, to have as much confidence in my body's ability to defend me as my magic, was at the top of my to-do list.

Right up there with finding some way to get rid of Sonja O'Dane permanently. Hopefully without turning Liam against me.

I tried to explain it to Charlotte who continued to scowl and play the deeply wounded bodywere.

Followed me to the gym I found in the phone book, still scowling.

Walked in with me, glaring.

She came with me, every time. Refused to help. To participate, despite the fact I knew what an amazing fighter she was. Could have learned a lot from her if she wasn't so damned stubborn about it. I felt terrible for the other people at the various gyms I tried who gave her a berth so wide she practically emptied every place when she walked in. It wasn't fair to the normals, not even a little. But I also knew better than to ask her to leave.

Three gyms later, the management at each spot took care of my wince-worthy worries for me by just asking us to leave. I was beginning to wonder if Charlotte would prevent me from finding the right place and if I'd have to be more firm about her staying home.

But when Sage smiled at me despite Charlotte's deadly emanations the first morning we met, standing to his full height with the biggest kettle bells I'd ever seen casually held in his very capable hands, I knew I'd found the place I was looking for. A little rough around the edges, full of bulky guys too busy looking at themselves to care what I did. Quiet. Dark.

Perfect.

"Good job, Syd," Sage said, bringing me back to the present. "Now double jab, uppercut, snap kick."

He'd taken one look at me that first day and seemed to know exactly what I needed.

"This isn't a normal gym," he said. "But you know that, right?"

I nodded, feeling a little intimidated as he towered over me, though more so by the instant zing of attraction I felt. Just what I needed, another boy to wrangle. But Sage's casual manner put me at ease as he set down the bells and offered his hand.

"Sage America," he said. Rolled his eyes in good humor. "Sad, right? My parents were late blooming hippies who thought it would be cool to curse their son for life."

I laughed and shook his hand. "Sydlynn Hayle," I said. "Same problem."

Instant friend.

Had to love it.

From that moment on, Sage was my go-to guy, though never in a forceful or bossy way. He let me try to figure stuff out on my own, fumbling with my hand wraps, my gloves, how to handle the heavy bag at the back of the room. Each time he gave me just enough space to feel frustrated before offering a hand, a simple explanation. Made me feel like I was valuable, important to him. His hands felt warm when he pulled the wraps tight. Confident when he laced up my small boxing gloves. Totally professional when he showed me how to keep the bag from taking me out instead of the other way around. Helped me find my rhythm, made sure I was comfortable.

Left me alone as if knowing that was what I really wanted.

Then showed me how it was supposed to be done when I hesitated.

I put the attention off to the fact it was his job and he was very good at it, but still, I looked forward to seeing him every morning.

Charlotte's sudden soft growl behind me caught my attention and I turned around.

"She'll be here soon," she said, her flat, unfriendly gaze locked on Sage.

He just grinned as she backed off, returning to her

place.

"Only two kind of people need a bodyguard," Sage said, casual and quiet. "I'm guessing you're not famous."

"Infamous," I said. "But nope."

He nodded. "Rich, then. Good for you." Like it was no big deal. I could really go for this guy—

Syd. Down girl.

"So I'll see you in the morning." He released the bag, gave me a salute. "Unless you're not busy tonight."

Whoa. That came out of left field. So much for professional. Still, he said it in such an offhand way, like it didn't matter, was just an offer.

And not unwelcome.

Because yeah, I did need another boy to worry about.

Was that real regret stirring, knowing I had to turn him down? The "she" Charlotte mentioned had to take priority.

"Can't tonight," I said. "But some other night, you bet."

Tell me I didn't just agree to go out with a normal.

Sage's little grin dimpled one stubbled cheek as he turned away. "That'll be great. I'm fairly new to town, just trying to settle in. It would be nice to have someone to hang around with."

Would it ever.

"See you, Syd." Sage tipped his chin at Charlotte with another smile before leaving me to clean up and go home.

Eyes front, girl. No staring at the wide shoulders walking in the other direction tapering down to a narrow waist over hips just visible at the hem of his loose shorts, the way the black fabric cupped his rock-hard ass—

I was going to girlfriend hell.

And I was okay with it.

Chapter Two

Sashenka Hensley tossed her heavy suitcase, the last of her belongings, onto the bed and spun in a circle, hugging herself and grinning. I grinned right back, as weird as it felt to have her living in Meira's room.

"This is perfect." My second ran her fingers over the pink walls, her magic sparkling out, tinting the paint as it traveled. A glittering wash converted the shade to a more demure taupe. "Well," she said with a wink, "now it's perfect."

I laughed as her magic completed its course with a final flare, job complete. "I never knew I could do that," I said, possibilities running through my mind. The house could use a spruce up.

Shenka unzipped her bag, tossing the top back. Charlotte's "she" ran one hand over the carefully arranged interior. I shook my head at how neat and orderly Shenka's stuff was, all folded and sorted by color and item. I sprawled on the bed and tried not to think of my little sister's absence as Shenka began removing her clothes from the case.

"Tallah was never happy with how the house looked," she said with an eye roll. Her sister, the leader of the Hensley coven, still wasn't very happy with me. Shenka had been her second, after all. And though I hadn't poached Shenka or anything, my best friend was looking for an out from her family and I was in desperate need of a second of my own.

She'd spent the last several weeks appeasing her sister with one final bout of family time. Though Shenka didn't have the Hensley power anymore, already tied to my coven, Tallah's need to spend time with her sister was one thing I understood completely.

Hurt my heart, knowing my own sister wanted nothing to do with me.

It was nice to have Shenka with us at last. A perfect fit. It still amazed me how easily Shenka integrated into the Hayle family. Everyone loved her. And she really was an excellent second. The way she handled every single person in the coven, with kindness and a personality I lacked, made Tallah's continuing coldness worth it.

"We'll have some fun," Shenka went on, a neat stack of folded t-shirts sliding into her drawer. With another gentle nudge of energy, she transformed the pale pink dresser into a lovely shade of apple green. "You won't recognize the place."

I never really thought about my surroundings all that much. We'd lived here for a long time, years, way longer than we'd ever stayed in one place before. Usually some kind of magical accident would arise to force the family to uproot in the middle of the night and move. But thanks to the dulled interest of the local townsfolk due to the presence of a Sidhe Gate, and the fact the Wild Hunt of the Sidhe slept under the back yard, we were settled in rather permanently.

A change of décor might be just the thing to shake the gloom I'd been feeling about Meira's absence in my life.

"It was lovely of Meira to let me use her room." Shenka kept her tone light, but we both knew "let" had nothing to do with it. After the disaster on Demonicon left Meira aged and addicted to a custom-designed brand of nectar, my sister's whole personality changed. I still worried she blamed me, even though she assured me it wasn't my fault, but hers. Our relationship remained strained and I'd only seen her once since our demon grandmother, Ahbi Sanghamitra, was interred in the Seat volcano after her state funeral.

Christmas. Awkward. She spent the entire time avoiding me. I knew she was under a lot of pressure, now that Dad named her heir to the Ruler throne, but it was a lot more than her new position keeping Meira from connecting with me again. She looked so different, her trips to Demonicon aging her as much as the nectar. Meira might have been eleven, eight years younger than me, but she looked twenty.

Spooky.

I gave her the space she wanted over the holidays and hadn't seen her since. Mom's suggestion Meira attend a European school seemed like a bad idea now. The girl I'd known and loved was gone, disappeared inside an intense young woman who kept her head down and refused to even talk to our demon cat, Sassafras.

Speak of the devil, he hopped his fat cat body onto the bed and sat, curling his fluffy tail around his paws as he observed Shenka's unpacking.

"How tidy," he said. "Syd, take notes."

Smartass cat.

Shenka smiled. "My mother was a neat freak," she said, using magic to float three sweaters on hangers to the walk-in closet, the metal hooks tinkling softly on the bar as they settled. "I guess I take after her."

"Perhaps you could assist Sydlynn with her room." Sassy's tail thrashed. "She's made a mess."

Things had shifted around quite a bit since Shenka signed on. Charlotte, my blonde-again bodywere, once camped in Meira's room as a temporary measure, now had my old room. So odd to walk up the stairs and not turn left, but right. Into Mom's room. Mine, now. Still. As much as I loved the ensuite bathroom, knowing I no longer had to share with anyone, it creeped me out using Mom's old space for my own. But Shenka argued it was the most logical choice of living arrangements and I knew she was right.

"I haven't finished unpacking yet," I said, swiping at Sass who swiped back with one silver paw.

"Ah," he said, amber eyes locked on me. "So that tornado that blew through earlier wasn't your fault?"

Okay, I was a slob. Big freaking deal.

Honestly? I struggled to spend much time in there. The large walk-in still smelled like lilacs, Mom's signature perfume. And so did the bathroom, a constant reminder of the ups and downs Mom and I endured over the years. Made me feel like she watched over my shoulder.

But the worst? She left me a little present, a small bottle of lilac essence with a note:

The Hayle family is in excellent hands.

Love, Mom.

And while I appreciated the sentiment, the bottle went right into the back of a drawer.

Gram burst through the open door, breaking my train of thought, giggling like a mad woman. Well, considering she hadn't completely recovered from her seventeen years in looney land, she really was still kind of crazy.

"Welcome home!" Gram lunged, not for me, but for

Shenka, hugging her tight, dancing the laughing second around in a circle before stepping back with a twinkle in her eye. Gram fished in the pocket of her sweater and pulled out—surprise, surprise—two pairs of fuzzy socks. One green, the other deep purple.

I had no idea what Gram's obsession was with fuzzy socks, but I had about a dozen pairs myself courtesy of her. Her own fluffy foot coverings today were bright blue with yellow stripes. Maybe it had to do with the fact they kept her in stealth mode, allowing her to sneak up on people. Her favorite.

Whatever the reason, Shenka smiled with real delight—how did she do that?—and accepted the offered socks.

"Thank you so much, Ethpeal." She sat instantly and slid her own crisp white socks from her feet, choosing the green ones, standing and wiggling her toes when she was done. "They're perfect."

Gram hugged her again while I grinned at the two of them. Shenka and I spent every weekend since she joined the family eight months ago traveling back and forth to Wilding Springs from Harvard, and the effort had really paid off. The coven adored her and, even better, were happy and content with me for once.

Imagine.

The subtle touch of someone entering the back yard triggered an old yearning I thought I'd erased. And though I knew it wasn't Quaid who waited for me there, a sad, pining part of me wished it was.

Always would.

I left Shenka and Gram to visit and unpack, Sassafras staring at me with those penetrating amber eyes of his, as though he knew exactly what I was thinking as I walked downstairs to talk to my visitor.

chapter three

Liam's arms were warm, the familiar scent of the earth mixed with fabric softener welcoming me as I exited the back door and stepped out, barefoot, into the cool grass to hug him.

I felt his lips press to the top of my head, his cheek settling against my hair as he pulled me close. Liam gave amazing hugs, whole body squeezes, which grounded and centered me. All thoughts of Quaid faded, all memories of Sage's delicious physique, as Liam's Sidhe power embraced me along with the strength of his arms.

"Hi," he whispered.

"Hi," I whispered back. Tilted my head to look up at him, so tall. He looked so much better than he had in the fall, recovered fully from the loss of Cian, his Sidhe soul after Ameline stole it in an effort to become maji. Even though I finally cornered and captured the evil witch, I still worried about her. Yes, she was in prison, awaiting trial, but she'd been in prison for months now. I knew the longer it took to finally get proceedings started, the more likely it would be Ameline, slippery as she was, could find a way to escape again.

What was taking the Council so long?

Liam's lips touched mine, hazel eyes sparking with green points of magic, cutting my thoughts off completely. Ameline who? There was nothing but thrumming earth magic under my skin, the heat of his body making my own temperature rise, the inhale of his breath.

Shaylee sighed in my head, my Sidhe princess welcoming him fully as my demon grumbled and sulked. I pushed her back. No way was she ruining this for me.

No, not her.

"There you are, kids!"

I jerked back from Liam at the same moment he stepped away from me, cheeks pink, a frustrated set to his shoulders. But he smiled as his mother clacked down the stone walk in her high heels, stylish hair and makeup perfectly put together. A hair stylist, Sonja always looked flawless, but there was lack of authenticity about her, which drove me bonkers.

That and the fact she was the clingiest helicopter mom I'd ever met. Liam wasn't alone two seconds and there was Sonja. I figured she blamed herself, not only for the loss of his father so many years ago to the Unseelie lordling, Venemeth, but thanks to her, Ameline was able to steal Liam's soul in the first place. Ever since I'd returned Cian to Liam, Sonja made herself a major pain in my ass.

"Hi, Mom." He never complained, always welcomed her, even at times like this. When we just wanted to be alone. I was ready to claw her eyes out and he was hugging her.

Momma's boy apron strings? Yeah, try a noose.

Sonja kissed his cheek, leaving a red lipstick imprint behind, a visible sign she'd claimed him as hers alone, before smiling at me so brightly I knew it was faked. I didn't bother smiling back, crossing my arms over my chest. "Hi, Syd."

Whatever.

Liam winced, but Sonja didn't react. Was she clueless or just didn't care? Either way, it totally sucked. I finally gave up Quaid, chose Liam. Even with the whole immortality thing, I'd finally chosen. Only to have his overbearing mother who refused to take the hint make it impossible for Liam and I to even consider a real relationship.

"I just finished buying you a brand new comforter and sheets." My, how relentless, considering he didn't live with her anymore. I expected nothing less from her but pure manipulation by now. Liam stiffened and dropped his arm from her shoulders. "Your room is ready, sweetie."

I might as well have not even existed as their old argument fired up.

"Mom," Liam said, voice cooling off considerably. "I'm not moving in with you. We've talked about this." Oh, they had. Over and over again, usually around me when Liam and I were meant to have "private time", time Sonja agreed to but never, ever honored. Did they have to do it again in front of me now? In my yard? I was really reconsidering this whole relationship thing with Liam. And it was all Sonja's fault.

"But, sweetie." Sonja reached for his hand. "I'm your mother. You really need to move home with me."

I snorted and almost turned to leave. Almost. The only thing keeping me? This was the only issue on which Liam stood his ground. And it gave me just a bit of hope knowing he refused to back down.

"My place is in the cavern." Liam pulled his hand away. "And that's the end of it."

Sonja's pout was meant to hurt him, stage two in her typical assault to achieve what she wanted. "Well," she said. "Your room is waiting for you. When you change your mind."

Dear elements, please cause harm to this woman before I was forced to take matters into my own hands.

"Well," I said, faking my own smile, "I have things to

do. Nice to see you both." That jab, joined with a bit of magic, was aimed straight at Liam. He winced and ducked his head before reaching for me.

"Don't go." The pleading in his eyes, in his voice, made me hesitate. Would have gone much further if he told his mother to leave. And I could have, too. Of course, I could have. Ordered her Unseelie ass off my property. But she was Liam's mother, and he already made it clear to me he loved and trusted her.

I didn't. Sure, Venner was off in the Sidhe realm at last, supposedly owing me a favor. But Hortense Spaft still floated around, his evil and hideous lieutenant, and since Sonja allowed herself be used before, my trust level was in the sewer when it came to her. Still, she was Liam's mother.

And while he'd never come out and said he put his mother first, that it was the package deal or nothing, I totally took the hint.

I loved him. But I wasn't sure he was worth it.

Damn it.

"I wanted to talk to you about your birthday." Liam's hazel eyes lit up again, a slow, sexy smile pulling at his wide lips. My body tingled immediately in response.

"A birthday!" Sonja practically put herself between us, so close to me I could see the powder clinging to the little hairs on her cheeks. "How exciting! We need to organize a party."

Yeah, the tingle was still there. But it now rippled with the need to murder the woman. My demon offered some violent alternatives while Shaylee huffed and puffed and demanded I just kill Sonja O'Dane already. Liam would never know. And she knew the perfect place to hide the body.

Oh dear.

Saved by my second. I heard the back door swing open just as I opened my mouth to tell Sonja I would never, ever, ever, ever attend anything remotely resembling a party if she organized it. Shenka entered my peripheral vision, smiling and taking my arm in a very firm grip.

"Mrs. O'Dane." Shenka backed me away a subtle step even as she took my place. "How lovely to see you." I knew Shenka despised the woman as much as I did. Okay, maybe not as much. She was at least able to pretend to be kind where I was way past any sophistry.

"Sashenka." Sonja backed up herself, arm hooking through Liam's. Possessively. Like she owned him.

Grrrr.

"Did I hear someone mention a party?" Shenka's face fell in artful sadness. "I'm sorry, but Syd's twentieth must be celebrated on Beltane, with the family. It's a closed ceremony, just for coven members. I'm sure you understand."

Liam's face fell, shoulders slumping as Sonja smiled

21

too quickly. Too happily.

"Certainly!" She pulled on Liam's arm. "How silly of us. Of course. Well, it was lovely seeing you. Come along, sweetie."

Liam turned, a tiny frown creasing his brow as he looked back over his shoulder at me.

I'm sorry, he sent. *This is nuts. I'll talk to her again, I promise.*

I didn't bother answering, just let him go, his irritating mother nattering in his ear all the way around the corner of the house and out of sight.

"You saved her life," I said.

Shenka sighed and hugged me.

"I know," she said. "Let's go bitch about her over chocolate."

I followed her inside, a hot ball of fury in my stomach.

As much as I loved Liam, if things didn't change, and now, I was done.

CHAPTER FOUR

Gram flipped a panini on the grill, crisping toast and hot chicken filling the kitchen with aromas so delicious my stomach growled despite my crabby mood.

As I took my plate, cheese bubbling out the edges of my sandwich, Gram caught my eye and snapped me once on the shoulder with her raised spatula.

"He's not strong enough for you," she said before pressing the lid down on the next sandwich with a loud hiss.

My teeth ground together as I turned my back on her, forgetting, under her challenging stare, I'd only moments before considered kicking Liam to the curb over his mother. But I'd chosen, hadn't I? Whether Gram liked it or not. And she'd never said anything like that about Liam before.

Not that I went looking for her opinion on my love life, thanks.

Shenka slid into a chair beside me, sympathy written all over her face as Sassafras hopped up on the table, crouching over his kitty paw placemat, amber eyes locked on the milk carton. "He'll get tired of his mother eventually," Shenka said, patting my hand. "He's just so sweet."

Gram snorted, tossing a second sandwich onto a plate and levitating it to Shenka who poured milk with her magic, Sass's bowl filling first before the carton poured a full glass for me. Charlotte took her usual place, standing by the doorway. Watching over us.

I wished she'd just come and eat. It wasn't like we were all that formal or anything. Far from it. And considering, if this were a normal house, all the magic in use would have been rather cool, she should have taken our casualness at face value.

Speaking of faces, I found myself forgetting my bodywere and glaring at the carton of milk with evil intent, wishing Sonja O'Dane's mug was on it.

Missing.

That would be awesome.

Gram joined us a moment later, her own steaming lunch following her as she claimed a chair, one fuzzy foot hooking the leg and pulling it over as her plate settled in front of her. A final plate landed in the empty space reserved for Charlotte. While the weregirl refused to join us, Gram never stopped trying.

I picked at the corner of the cooling cheese, a sour taste in my mouth killing my appetite.

"Sweet will get him nowhere." Gram took a giant bite, breathing out steam through her open mouth before she chewed aggressively, eyes locked on mine. "And will hold you back, girl."

Wow. "Since when did you develop this hate-on for Liam?" First I'd heard of it from her. A whiny voice in my head complained it wasn't fair even as I smothered it with a burst of anger.

No whining. Never again.

"No one said anything about hate," Sassafras said, looking up from the plate of tuna Shenka set in front of him. "But Liam isn't as strong as he could be. Not his fault, considering how he's been raised." Sass took a quick lap of milk before sniffing the fish. "But we all know he's never been allowed to develop to his full potential."

Sonja again. Sheesh.

"Listen to me, Sydlynn Thaddea Hayle." Gram never used my real name, let alone my full one. I found myself sitting up straighter, petulance long gone, goosebumps rising on my skin. "That boy has a huge heart and he loves you."

But.

"But." She shook her head, white hair floating around

her head in wisps like a puffy halo. Almost comical, considering Gram was no angel. "He doesn't have the strength you need. He'll never stand up to you. He'll cave, over and over again."

"I'm not that bossy." Yeah. Stop laughing.

Gram arched an eyebrow, a terrible little grin pulling at her lips. "You're a Hayle," she said. "We invented bossy."

Shenka giggled, covered it with a cough while Sassafras snorted milk.

Even Charlotte's normally blank expression twitched in humor.

Traitors.

"If you end up with that boy," Gram said, sitting back, one foot bouncing violently at the end of her crossed leg, "you'll turn him into a weakling yes-man. And you know it."

"I like nice and sweet," I shot back, pushing my plate away as my anger rose. "And there's nothing wrong with a partner who says yes."

You know she's right, my vampire whispered.

Shut up, I snapped back.

"This coven, your responsibilities, they will try to devour you, girl." Gram's voice dropped, tone sad and hollow. "Trust me. I know."

Okay, fair enough. She lost seventeen years of her sanity, all for the coven. But I wasn't her.

"I can't pick who I love," I said.

Oh, Syd.

Liar, liar.

Gram's steady gaze told me she knew I was full of crap. "You'll need support," she said, reaching across the table to me. "Shenka will be part of that." My second nodded quickly, looking back and forth between us. "Sassafras." The demon cat's eyes flared with fire. "But they can only do so much. Sass's job is to watch over your heirs. Shenka's is supporting the coven. Yours is keeping the family safe. And your mate..." Gram squeezed my fingers. "Your mate's job is to be there when you need someone strong to lean on, who'll challenge you when you're being an idiot. Push you when you want to quit. Love you, no matter what." Was that a tear in her eye? My heart constricted as I thought about my grandfather, what I knew of Ivan Dumont. His betrayal of our family. Of Gram.

"Ethpeal is one hundred percent correct." Sassafras finished his bowl of milk, swiping at his whiskers with one paw. "I've seen generations of Hayle witches come and go and one thing is certain—a strong mate means a happy coven."

Anger flared inside me, the need to defend Liam so powerful a snap of magic shattered the plate under my uneaten lunch. Shenka jumped with a tiny cry, but neither Gram nor Sassafras so much as flinched.

Temper, Sydlynn, my vampire sent.

Whatever.

"I'd like to know why you think you have the right to say anything," I snapped at Gram, unreasonable anger driving me to bitterness. Damn her, I'd chosen! "Your husband was a family traitor."

Oh. Crap. Damn it. I hadn't said that out loud. Had I?

This time Sass did react, a hiss of fury sending sparks of amber magic over his puffed-up fur as he glared at me.

"Watch what you say," he snarled.

Shenka didn't move, barely breathed, staring at me, as though waiting for an explosion. But Gram just sighed and nodded. "You're right," she said. "What do I know?" She stood, taking her plate with her, half a sandwich untouched as the temperature in the room seemed to drop to zero. I shivered, hugging myself, wanting to take it back. Gram didn't deserve to be treated this way. She was always up front with me, always honest. And I knew absolutely, without question, she had my best interest and that of the coven, at heart at all times.

Perhaps you're so angry, my vampire sent, *because you know she's right.*

Twinge.

I didn't get to deliver the sharp comment on the tip of my mind. I jerked in response to the sudden jab of another mind reaching for mine, gasping out loud as I clutched at my head. Even through the powerful family wards, the pointed attack made it through. I watched Gram spin with a frown of concern in the periphery of my vision, Shenka reaching for me, Sassafras's magic surging toward me, Charlotte's eyes flickering from blue to wolf as she left her post to come to my side. But I lost them all as I balled up my power in preparation to fight back.

Syd! I knew that voice, the power behind it. Not an attack. I pulled back just in time, only a heartbeat before I blew Mia's mind into a gazillion fragments.

What's wrong? My body trembled with releasing tension before she seized me in a surge of desperate energy fading almost as quickly as it rose.

Help me Syd please help they're taking it and I can't stop them and I don't know what to do please help they're dying—

I was losing her, Mia's touch failing, falling away, weaker by the second. Gram's power linked with mine, Shenka's right behind her, Sassafras's demon magic pushing us further as I wound myself around the last of Mia's touch and held onto her.

A single image made it through, from Mia's perspective, a slow tumble to the right as she fell onto polished marble stairs, dark shapes looming over her before she slipped away from me.

With one last whisper.

Please help—

I dropped out of the connection, already on my feet,

all thoughts of Liam gone.

The Dumont coven was under attack.

CHAPTER FIVE

I ran for the back door, reaching for the veil I knew I wouldn't be able to access until I left the property and the family wards, only to feel someone's hand on my arm. I spun around, panic fighting against Shenka who shook her head, face grim.

"I have to help her." I tried to pull free, but Shenka's fingers refused to open, her grip on my sleeve keeping me still. Gram and Sassafras stood behind her, the demon cat clutched to my grandmother's chest. No surprise, Charlotte stood on my left, my constant shadow ready to join me without question.

"You have to play by the rules." My second's words chilled the fire burning inside me, the need to rush off and save Mia. My old friend, the leader of the Dumont coven, hadn't been in close touch in a long time, not since the debacle at Harvard when she'd lost her boyfriend, Rupe, to Ameline's manipulations. Not to mention how some of the members of her coven had been associated with Ameline's plan.

I'd done my best to support Mia, to help her cement her rule of her coven, but in this case, Gram was absolutely right when she'd said ages ago Mia wasn't strong enough to run her own family. Her power crippled when she was a baby by a mother who was just trying to protect her, Mia spent her whole life knowing she was different, but unable to access the magic she craved. I always worried she would crack under the strain, considering the corruption in her coven.

But I never expected the Dumonts to fall under attack.

Shenka shook me a little, dark eyes intense. "Miriam needs to be informed."

Right. The rules thing. Mom warned me last fall I stomped on thin ice with the Council. She'd done her best to protect me in the past, but by pushing the limits of the law, I put myself in a position of interest.

This was different, though. I wasn't meddling. "Mia asked for my help," I said, urgency rising again. "I have to go."

Shenka nodded quickly. "Of course you do," she said. "But you tell your mother, first."

Gram tossed Sass into my arms, the silver Persian's

claws hooking on my t-shirt. "Do it," she said.

Mom. I threw my power at my mother, catching an image of her looking up, startled and angry, from her desk.

Sydlynn Thaddea—

I didn't let her finish. Pummeled her with what I'd just gone through. Mom's anger disappeared in a flash, the feeling of her rising and moving quickly feeding my own desperate need to act.

Go, she sent. *I'll be there shortly with Enforcers. You know where to find her?*

Following her call. I spun on Shenka and Gram, Sassafras tucked against my chest. "Watch the family," I said before turning and sprinting across the yard and into the edge of the park, tearing a massive hole in the veil the moment I crossed over the family wards.

Quaid, Sass sent as we leaped from the other side, my feet landing on a manicured lawn, Charlotte releasing a soft hiss as we emerged at the end of a long, cobbled drive leading up to a massive mansion, more castle than house.

Right. I reached for the Enforcer trainee, knowing he'd want to help Mia if he could, though I knew the siblings were as estranged as Mia and I.

Why was I surprised to feel him nearby? More shock, the Dumont family wards were down.

No, not down.

Gone.

I slipped into the veil again rather than run what looked like a half mile to the front door, stepping out into a large foyer of marble and dark stone, a thick, purple carpet soft under my feet, climbing the staircase. Charlotte's deep growling cut through the stillness, punctuated by the sound of crying. I almost tripped over a fallen woman, her angular face characteristic of her Dumont heritage, skin pale, eyes closed. Sassafras leaped from my arms as I looked around in horror. The foyer was filled with the fallen, Dumonts all, from the look of them, some staring empty-eyed at the ceiling, others groaning softly, weeping.

But the worst was the young woman resting in the arms of the black-robed Enforcer six stairs up. Mia sobbed in Quaid's arms, her black Goth makeup trailing down her white cheeks. I choked on disbelief, a horrible feeling of dread rising in my chest as I followed Sassafras who streaked up the steps to land in Mia's arms.

She hugged him, the sound of him purring reaching me long before I knelt beside her, my demon cat's particular brand of comfort vibrating through her body. Mia looked up at me, ice blue eyes huge before she lunged toward me, pulling away from Quaid to embrace me, Sassafras squashed, but still purring, between us.

"Oh, Syd!" She clung to me, sobbing harder despite Sassy's comforting magic.

I hugged her back, reaching for her power.

Felt it, puny, small.

My entire body shuddered as I understood at last what happened, terror for my own family clenching my muscles tight as I reached for Gram.

It's gone. I could barely whisper in my mind. *The Dumont power. Just. Gone.*

I had no idea how. Didn't know it was possible.

But there wasn't a trace of the old family's magic anywhere.

Gram touched me, understood. Gasped before cursing. *We're gathering the coven*, she sent. *Everyone is safe. So far. Keep us informed.*

I met Quaid's eyes, registered the hurt as he leaned away from his sister. I reached for him with one hand even as Mia fell back again, grasping at me and her brother at the same time.

The air around me exploded all at once, shocks of blue magic erupting as dozens of Enforcers suddenly appeared overhead. Mom burst into view, landing with a thud on the step below us, leaning over Mia as she reached for the girl. Mia fell into Mom's embrace, shuddering uncontrollably, Sassafras slipping free, still purring, but shaking his head at me.

No amount of comfort magic would help Mia. Not now.

Maybe not ever again.

I caught glimpses of Enforcers gathering the fallen Dumonts, but kept my attention on Mom. Her blue eyes met mine as she rocked Mia, her power engulfing the girl even as she touched my mind.

The family?

I hugged her mentally. *Safe. For now.*

Mom seemed to relax a fraction, only enough I noticed, knowing her so well.

"Mia," Mom said. "You must tell us what happened."

The Dumont leader gasped a shuddering breath before absolute hate crossed her face, transforming her from grief to evil in a breath.

"She did this," Mia snarled. "Ameline."

I shook my head immediately even as Mom answered.

"That's impossible," Mom said. "Ameline is in prison. And has been for months. You know this."

Mia's whole body bucked as she jerked free of Mom, vibrating with her hate, feet pattering against the floor as her heavy boots thudded into the thick carpet.

"She did this!" Her scream echoed through the giant foyer, catching the attention of the Enforcers who tended to her family. Everyone stared as Mia lurched to her feet, balls of flickering lavender magic appearing and disappearing around her hands as the meager amount of power she still had access to struggled to do her bidding.

"Rupe was here." Mia's voice dropped, a deep hiss.

Her old boyfriend vanished with Ameline after she

tried to steal my vampire essence. So I could understand why Mia was so convinced. But I delivered Ameline into custody myself. Fear lanced through me as I turned to Mom.

She is in custody. Right?

Mom didn't answer. Didn't have a chance. Mia spun on Quaid, grasping him by the front of his robe, the magic lighting the fabric on fire.

"You find her," Mia shrieked, "and you kill Ameline Benoit for stealing our family magic!"

chapter six

I stood back, trying to stay out of the way, the horror of the circumstance still weighing on me as I watched Enforcers carry the injured—and the dead—to various parts of the house. More and more fallen Dumonts appeared, from rooms scattered all over the giant mansion. I knew the family was large, hundreds of members, but I had no idea they all lived together in a fortress like this.

No way I could handle having my coven around me 24/7. No. Way.

Quaid stood next to me, head down, face drawn into a tight scowl. I knew he had to be lost in the demand Mia made of him. It took me a little while to break out of my own shock, but once I did, my hand crept into his and he accepted what fraction of comfort I had to offer without question.

Our magic linked, flowed together, his tie to the Hayle coven still as strong as ever, though now buried under his growing Enforcer power. I dreaded the day he accepted his place as a full Enforcer, knowing, despite the fact I'd set him free from me, I'd cry over his loss when he finally severed our last connection.

Pender Tremere, the Enforcer leader, strode with ponderous concern to our side, one hand landing on Quaid's shoulder as he bowed his head to me. The air over us continued to burst and ripple with magic as more and more Enforcers arrived, others leaving, the rush of activity making me feel dizzy and starting a headache behind my right eye.

"Thank you for coming, Coven Leader." Pender turned to Quaid. "Perhaps you'd like to stay with your sister?"

Quaid shook himself, breaking our touch as he straightened his shoulders. "I'm here to serve, sir."

Pender smiled sadly and dropped his hand from Quaid's shoulder. "I know," he said. "In that case, I ask you to please attend to the Dumont leader, if you would, trainee."

Quaid's face spasmed in pain, rippling through his magic to me.

"Yes, sir," he said.

"What will happen now?" I hugged myself, looking around, wincing from the scent of death and the cold feeling of the house, the pressure of so much grief and loss sucking at my spirit. Though most of the family was now behind closed doors, under care, the place still had the feeling of a giant refugee camp.

Pender looked around too, lines etched deeply in his narrow face. "I don't know," he said, ever so softly, as though he wasn't aware he spoke. "Nothing like this has ever happened before. We'll be here to guard the family, naturally. Until some resolution can be found."

He didn't have to say there wasn't much left to protect.

Mom strode toward us, face calm, emotionless, though I knew her better than that. She did the whole Council Leader thing way better than I would ever play my role and I wondered if she'd teach me how to hide my emotions so I didn't have to feel like my pessimism was only adding to the problem.

"That's the last of them, at least as far as we know." Mom's fingers brushed my cheek, the momentary contact allowing me in, to feel how weary and sad she was before she dropped her hand. "According to Council rolls, there should be three hundred and seventy six members."

Holy. Our coven of just over a hundred felt small in comparison.

"Any outside the premises?" Pender sounded all official again. Mom had that effect on most people, despite the kindness she showed those beneath her.

"Some." She reached out and took Quaid's hand. "They've been located and brought back."

Quaid's chocolate eyes flashed with blue power. "How many lost?"

Mom hesitated, long enough I knew the answer wasn't good.

Not that losing even one witch was okay, Dumonts or not. Yes, they'd been a thorn in our sides for a long time. But bygones were bygones as far as I was concerned. After the death of Odette, their misguided leader, the worst I had from the Dumont family was the occasional irritation from Mia's cousins, Jean Marc and Kristophe.

No, I didn't like the Dumont family. But no coven deserved this fate.

No witch.

And from the tension around Mom's eyes, the number ran high.

"One hundred and forty three," Mom said as Quaid's brow tightened, my own stomach clenching. "Survivors."

Dear. Elements. Almost two thirds of the coven...

Dead.

"So far," Mom said. Winced. "Some are still touch and go."

I quivered, reached for Gram, felt her support me as tears welled, my throat tightening. For the Dumonts, but more so, for us.

Who had done this? And why?

More importantly, were other covens at risk?

I had to assume so. "Mom," I said. Didn't have to finish.

She nodded quickly, her mask falling away as rage flickered over her face. "I know," she said. "We'll find out who did this. I swear it. And they will pay."

While I appreciated her sentiment, the pessimist in me was still alive and well. Whoever did this, whoever attacked the Dumonts, brought a powerful coven to its knees. And while yes, Mia wasn't the strongest leader, the Dumont family was generations old and one of the strongest in North America. If they'd fallen so easily...

Choke.

"It could have been Ameline," Quaid said, voice gravel over coals, burning with fury. "Not directly, but she could have had a hand in it."

Mom didn't say anything, but she had to be thinking the same thing. "She'll be questioned," Mom said.

"Mia mentioned Rupe." My normal friend, the Goth guy I'd known as Blood, who I'd reconnected with at Harvard only to have him stripped away by Ameline. A tug of guilt reminded me I hadn't thought of him in ages. Or continued to look for him after my initial hunt for him failed when he disappeared. "So you could be right, Quaid."

Mom let his hand go, stepping back, mask in place once again. "As I said, she'll be questioned."

"Let me talk to her." Ameline had been trying to lure me in for months, sending endless notes, claiming she needed to see me. I ignored her, but maybe it was time to take her up on her invitation.

Mom's flat, cold expression shut me down well before I could offer further.

"I will handle Miss Benoit," she said. "It's time for the Hayle coven leader to return home."

She said what?

Let me handle this, Mom sent, mental tone sharp and rigid.

Mia asked for my help, I sent back, with my own razor edge. *Directly.*

I know, Mom sent. *That's why you haven't been arrested.* She did *not* just say that to me. *But your initial invitation was just that. Initial. It's now my job to handle this.*

Mom didn't wait for me to answer, spinning and striding off. I watched her go, seething, my horror turned to fury aimed at the back of her head.

Pender bowed to me before walking after Mom. Quaid turned to me, dark eyes full of churning emotions, as powerful as mine.

I'll keep you posted. His magic slid around me, pulled me close, the intensity of his need to act firing me up, sending my demon into a cycle of snarling and snapping even as she reached back, tightening the connection.

There again, the tingle, the pull. The touch I'd

thought lost to me. Still there, calling.

His hair felt soft, thick under my hands as I clasped the back of his neck, welcoming his lips as he bent over me. A burst of power surged between us, heating my body to boiling as his lips devoured mine, hands hot where they pressed to my t-shirt. I sank into him, and he into me, our bodies locking together as we both took what we needed.

Passion. Support. Promise.

Quaid pulled away first, leaving me panting, my demon snarling at him to come back, to stay with us. A need like I'd never known burned in his eyes, a need I knew very well.

Too well.

Quaid let me go, stepping back while I did the same, the touch of his Enforcer magic coming between us.

"I'm sorry," he said.

"I'm not." It came out fierce, full of pain.

Quaid hesitated. "How's Liam?"

Bastard.

"How's Payten?" Oh, the pain we brought each other.

Quaid straightened, nodded.

And me? Well. I walked away.

chapter seven

It brought me at least a little satisfaction to ignore Mom's direct order. Rather than leave immediately, I pushed my boundaries and went looking for Mia.

She had my demon cat, after all. And I was more than a little attached to his fuzzy butt.

Charlotte padded softly behind me, footfalls louder than usual. As though she wanted me to know she was there.

I stopped to face her, meeting her blue eyes, flickering with the wolf inside her. She hovered closer than usual, body loose and liquid.

While I went tense when I prepped for battle, Charlotte was the opposite. As though knowing she headed for trouble triggered extra fluidity.

Charlotte was ready for a fight. As long as it wasn't with me, we were fine. When her wolf surged to the surface and took over for a moment, I knew it wasn't me she wanted to thrash. But she threw in a little nod anyway.

Just so I'd know it.

It couldn't have been easy for her, being in this house. The Dumonts held her and her pack captive here for who knew how long. Thralled and forced to protect Odette and her hideous bloodline, Charlotte must have memories she wanted to erase. And since I knew the lengths this family used to be willing to go to when they wanted something, I could imagine Charlotte's life hadn't been easy.

Not even a little bit.

The guilt I felt because she traded ownership by the Dumonts for servitude to me didn't help much. And even though I would have loved to talk to her about it, previous attempts to find out more about her past failed. And she gave me no indication such questions would meet with anything more than silence and stubbornness.

Instead of continuing to beat my head against that particular brick wall, I focused on finding my demon cat. We found Sassafras curled up next to Mia in a large, four poster bed carved from black stone laced with purple crystals. Her room was huge, reminding me of my old bestie, Alison, and the massive mansion she grew up in. Guilt twanged at the thought of the dead cheergirl, but I didn't have time for her or her memory now. Besides, this place was much more ostentatious, as bad as the rest of the mansion/castle, with furniture clearly imported from France and heavy black curtains better off on a horror movie set than a bedroom. The whole space gave me the creeps, the fact Mia felt so weak and lost not helping matters any.

The sound of Sassy's purring finally lulled me, and I wondered if he'd been eavesdropping on my conversation with Mom. I knew Gram probably had and wouldn't put it past my demon Persian to do the same.

No privacy for Syd. Not ever.

Mia opened her eyes as I entered, two Enforcers flanking the bed coming to attention. I waved them off and approached as if I was supposed to be there, hadn't been ordered to leave, sitting next to my friend. Not looking at Quaid who stood with his back to me, staring out the slit in the curtains.

Mia reached for my hand, huge blue eyes achingly wide, full of so much agony I felt my throat tighten all over again.

"Syd," she cried. "What am I going to do?"

I leaned over her and hugged her, feeling her desperation through her embrace. "We'll figure this out," I said, that same fierceness I'd experienced with Quaid rechanneling into rage and determination. "I promise."

She nodded against my shoulder before falling back. "I had to call you," she whispered. "You were the only one I could trust."

Wow. Sob. And here I thought she hated me, had cut me out of her life for all these long months. I always considered Mia my friend, even when she'd broken down after I tried to support her, had advised her to prune the bad apples from her coven when I didn't know if she had the strength to do it. She came looking for my help then, too, and I'd given her what assistance I could without being arrested. She cut me off after that, hadn't followed through, left me with the impression I wasn't welcome in her life anymore. But knowing how much she thought of me made things ten times worse. Could I have prevented this, helped her more, supported her if I'd just pushed a little harder, been a better friend?

Don't be an idiot, Gram sent in a tight burst of connection.

Right. No coven interference. Still.

"I wouldn't have let him in." Mia sagged, a doll missing her stuffing. "If I'd know, Syd, I never would have."

"Rupe?" My forehead pinched before I forced myself to calm. She didn't need me freaking on her. She was enough of a mess herself.

Be supportive for once, Syd. Sheesh.

"He just showed up at the door." She smiled and cried all at once before her face crumpled and she coughed out a series of barking sobs before falling still again. "He told me he loved me." Could the whole situation be more horrible? More terrible than this? "I let him in. And then..."

"And then?" I didn't want to know. But I had to. Needed to protect my family.

Selfish, selfish.

Damned right.

"Will he kill her for me?" Mia's body trembled violently as she clutched at my hand. "Quaid. Will he kill Ameline, do you think?"

I glanced sideways at his tall, broad back, the way his shoulders twitched. How she spoke of him as if he wasn't even here. More sympathy, more pain. "If she's guilty," I said, absolutely believing it. "I'll kill her myself."

Mia wailed softly before letting my hand go. "This is worse," she whispered. "So much worse than before. You remember?"

I knew exactly what she meant. When she was powerless. I'd been there, too. Back when things were simpler, when she was the Goth girl Pain, her boyfriend Blood at her side, high school and bullies and a séance waking some of her buried magic. Magic that only returned to her when the Sidhe soul she carried forced her way to the surface the night the Wild Hunt attacked.

The night she turned eighteen and her mother's protections shattered.

I knew how she felt. But I didn't, not really, did I? I'd

been cut off from my personal magic, from my demon when Demetrius Strong took her from me. The power Gram left inside me as a baby smothering my magic to keep itself safe. But I wasn't coven leader then. Didn't have access to all that power. The memory of stepping inside the mansion of the Brotherhood rose instead. All power gone, cut off.

Blind, deaf, dumb, silent.

Okay, yeah. I did know.

Shudder.

"Now I understand what it's supposed to feel like, it's so much worse." Mia's face shone slick with tears while I nodded and wished I could just run away and let someone else comfort her before I broke down and sobbed with her.

She rolled her head to the side, looking away from me, mouth gaping open as she wept into her black velvet pillow and I knew, deep down, my damaged and weak-minded friend finally reached her limit.

Mia Dumont was broken and there was nothing I could do about it.

Time to go. Sassafras set one paw in my lap.

So he had heard Mom's order. *How can I just leave her like this?* No, I wasn't responsible.

Was I?

Let your mother handle it, Sassafras sent. *We have our own coven to protect.*

Fear rippled through me before I pushed him gently aside and bent over Mia. Yes, my family had to take priority. But I also refused to just leave my friend after she asked for my help again.

Maybe for the last time.

"Mom's asking me to leave," I said. She turned her head back, blue eyes dead, drained of emotion at last. "But if you tell her it's okay, I can stay. Support you."

A flicker of something shone in her gaze a moment. Hope? I doubted it. Maybe a long-lost distant cousin. Mia seemed far removed from finding a shred of hope. And then, it died, leaving her shell to shake her head a little.

"Thank you for being here," she said, in the voice of an automaton.

I hugged her, felt her collapse under my embrace, hollow and lost, before turning away, leaving her there though my guilt drove me near to the breaking point, and abandoned my friend to her fate.

chapter eight

It was a slower ride home, though it still only took seconds for the veil to dump the three of us at the edge of our property. I crossed over into the yard, welcoming the feeling of the family wards as they embraced me, the coven's power surging forward to suck me in and wrap me up in a blanket of magic protection.

There was a time I would have resisted such an embrace. Not today. I needed all the hugs I could get.

The Wild Hunt slept peacefully beneath my feet as I crossed the bright green grass to the back door. I shuddered to think what would happen if the Hayle family magic was stolen. Gwynn ap Nudd and his riders would rise, devouring the plane in storm and disaster.

But I'd be long gone, so it wouldn't matter to me, I guessed. Because anyone trying to take my family's power would do it over my dead and mangled body.

Gram waited for me at the back door, holding it wide for Sass and Charlotte, her arm slinging around my waist as I let them go ahead of me, the screen door thudding shut behind us, Gram steering me toward the kitchen.

Shenka sat at the table, gaze far away as Sassafras hopped up to his place, Charlotte pacing to look out the kitchen door as though expecting an imminent attack.

My second came back to us with a soft shudder before rising to hug me, face wreathed in concern.

"How's Mia?"

I filled them in, knowing Gram already had the scoop thanks to the bond we shared through the family magic. She was still part leader, after all, though she'd been siphoning more and more of the power to me over the last little while. Since I'd chosen Shenka, actually. Still, it didn't keep her from poking around in my head whenever she felt like it.

Nosy, old—

"As much as I hate to agree with her," Gram cut off my train of thought. Convenient. "I have to agree with Miriam."

I slumped into a chair and bobbed a nod. "I know," I said. "It's wrong, Gram. Mia needs us now, more than ever. But coven law is coven law." Even when it didn't make much sense, the laws of our society were the fabric holding us all together. Or something equally as ridiculous.

Shenka tapped her finger-tips against the table, dark skin flushed with worry. "I tried to get through to Tallah," she said. "But I couldn't reach her."

Gram grunted, dropping into her own seat. "The pair of you stay out of it," she said, jabbing one index finger first at Shenka, then at me, a prod of magic joining her gesture. "Besides, as far as I'm concerned, it's a problem solved."

Gram's dislike—okay, utter hate—for the Dumont family wasn't exactly a big secret. Thanks to Odette and her puppet sister, Naudia, Gram lost her husband, her sanity and almost her life. But there were bigger implications here I couldn't move beyond.

"You know whoever stole the Dumont magic must have an agenda." Gram wouldn't meet my eyes. Of course she knew. "And they now have control of one of the most powerful coven cores on our continent." For all I knew, in the world. Gram crossed her arms over her chest, jaw set. "And no matter what they've done, what their leaders have done, no family deserves what happened, Gram." I reached for her, forced her arms down by digging my fingers in between her clenched grip, took her hand as she finally relented and thudded one heel against the chair leg in unhappiness. I opened to both of them, Shenka included, and let them feel what I felt, see what I saw. Gram didn't flinch. She'd been watching. But Shenka's small cry of grief softened my grandmother's hardness until she sagged and sighed.

Faded blue eyes met mine. "What do you want to do?"

"Call the coven." I sat back, chewing my bottom lip. "Have either of you told them what happened?"

Mutual head shakes. "We didn't know," Shenka said while Gram grimaced and winked. Bratski. "But there were inquiries when we tightened the wards."

"They need to know what's going on." I reached out, down through the network, feeling Gram support me, her approval of my choice solidifying my resolve. Would it cause panic? Probably. At least at first. But they deserved to know. A forewarned coven was a forearmed coven.

They reached for me, eager and curious. I did my best to mask my worry, though I could tell from some of them I didn't succeed fully.

The warmth of the family embraced me as I connected down to the last member.

I'm calling a meeting. A tiny part of me shivered, regretted. Second guessed. How many times would I drag my family through disaster after mess after impending doom? And yet, was it fair to keep them in the dark? *Mandatory attendance. Immediately.*

I tempered my words with love and kindness, but allowed out enough urgency they responded with instant agreement. The basement door beckoned as I stood and retreated below, descending the stairs with Gram behind me, Charlotte following, Sassafras bounding ahead while Shenka remained behind, mind linked to mine, to welcome the family as they arrived at our door.

I stopped in the center of the pentagram, gathered myself, shielding my thoughts from everyone, drawing on the family magic as I stared down at the symbols etched in the concrete floor.

Magic flowed through the house as the family crossed the wards, in twos and threes, within moments of my call. I felt them filling the basement, heard the soft murmur of their voices, but kept myself apart, trying to decide how to tell the people who looked to me to keep them safe I had no idea if I could. For all I knew, every coven was now at risk. And though I would fight for them to my last breath, the thought of even one of my family dying—let alone in the numbers Mia lost—closed my throat and made it hard to focus.

Full complement. Shenka's smooth, warm mental voice touched my mind. *Everyone is here.*

I turned, lifting my head, wrapping myself in the power of the family, letting my shielding drop and welcoming them to me. The coven swayed, men, women, children staring, concern growing though their support didn't waver. Gone was the family fearful of my leadership. Fearful of what might happen. Instead, they offered strength and utter faith and, for the first time since Mia reached for me, I felt my heart sigh and unclench.

We'd be fine. No matter what happened.

We were Hayles.

"My family," I said, tears rising in my eyes as I hugged them tight. "I have terrible news." I filled them in quickly, letting them into my memories as I shared the plight of the Dumont coven. They gasped and wept and embraced each other, but their faith never wavered. Not even a bit. Not even when one of the Lawrence sisters, little Estelle with her perfect twinset and comfortable shoes, met my eyes and spoke the unspeakable.

"Are we at risk?" Her voice sounded strong, level. Confident. Her twin, Esther, held her hand, face as composed as her sister's.

"No one knows," I said. "It's possible this was a singular attack against the Dumonts."

"Perhaps a coven to coven attack?" Esther's tone matched Estelle's.

"Perhaps." I met Gram's eyes, saw the pride there, tied to her own faith. "But I doubt it. We must be realistic about this." Everyone shifted, a hundred hearts pounding, a hundred souls shifting together. "There is a very good chance the Dumont coven was only the beginning. Any family could be next."

They accepted the truth without falling to pieces. Wicked. From the way they looked at me, that was my doing. So who was going to hold me together?

We will. My vampire's whisper joined the hum of my demon, Shaylee's soft sigh and the thrum of the family magic.

Right. Never alone.

"I want to offer support to the Dumont coven." I felt them recoil, Gram among them, but pursued my thought before they could reject it. "I know Odette was our enemy. But they have a new leader. And she needs us now. Her family does, what's left of it." They shuddered as one, relented. All but Gram who fixed me with her piercing eyes. "I have an ulterior motive. Naturally." I let myself smile, a weak and frail thing, but enough they relaxed into my reasoning. "If this threat is coming for us, I want as much information as possible. Firsthand accounts from the Dumont family." My people sighed, swayed, nodding and welcoming my suggestion now. "I won't make any of you go. But I'm asking for volunteers."

The twins came forward immediately, a dozen or so others, couples with no children, singles. My chest tightened as I realized they chose among themselves, those who could be lost without too much effect to the whole. I swallowed the lump of love and bitterness before nodding and reaching for Mom.

The Hayle coven offers support to the Dumont coven. Her mind flinched from mine as the whole family pushed behind me, their agreement undeniable. *As long as Mia agrees.* And, in a private aside: *I'm not asking permission.*

Mom's mental voice scraped over mine. *Very well*, she sent. *But only if the coven leader agrees.*

As I released Mom, my mind worked over her words. Actually, the Dumonts weren't a coven anymore, were they? Their family magic was gone. And Mia, almost powerless, wasn't their leader.

A technicality, Gram sent. *But we'll exploit it if we need to.*

You agree? I watched the family break focus, talking among themselves, knew I'd have a lot of people to speak to individually in the next few hours, but allowed them time to be together.

Not completely. Irritation tinted her gruff mental tone. *But you're right about digging for info. Just don't ask me to lift a finger to help.*

Wouldn't dream of it. I almost laughed, would have if things weren't so horribly serious. *Besides, I have another job for you.*

She bobbed her head, white hair wavering. *Figured*, she sent. *Just be careful, girl. It's a fine line you're dancing along. One false step and you won't need to worry about the power thieves.*

I hated that she was right.

CHAPTER NINE

Hurry up and wait was never so agonizing. After Mia's almost eager acceptance of Hayle coven support, the small group of family I transferred settled in to help with healing and protection. Mia wasn't on her feet yet, not making an appearance when I finally left my small group behind. But not much time had passed, only a few hours, so I wasn't really all that surprised.

The real agony came over the next two days, waiting, wondering. I paced the house, certain I'd wear holes in the floors, wanting to be there myself, but knowing Mom would immediately pull the plug if I pushed her too hard. Esther and Estelle did a great job contacting me at regular intervals, but neither of them had much to report.

It seems not just the family power was taken, Estelle sent early that first evening. *Either that, or the witches in this coven are naturally weak, only powerful because of their family magic.*

Possible, Esther sent. *Whatever the case, with the loss of the family's power, not one of the witches here will be capable of much alone. And even were they to try to form a coven again, with what limited power they have available, there is no way that magic could support a family this size.*

Even reduced as they are, Estelle sent. *Agreed.*

I let them go after each exchange, growing more frustrated by the moment. Shenka's attempts to reach her sister continued to fail and I began to wonder if Mom had something to do with it.

How much had she told the other covens, if anything at all? I wouldn't put it past her to block our attempts to talk outside our family if she didn't want what happened to become common knowledge just yet. Still, it was pretty damned selfish, considering the growing worry bowing Shenka's shoulders.

And as far as I was concerned, everyone needed to know. Everyone.

When the sun set on the third day with no answers, silence from Mom and Tallah and my nerves frazzled to a crispy edge thanks to the constant vigilance we maintained, I finally had enough. Gram must have known how close I was to my breaking point, because as I slammed down my fork and opened my mouth to tell her I was going to the Dumonts, she casually sipped her water before saying, "Why don't you go check on our people?"

Shenka choked on her dinner before flashing me a tight grin, one fading as fast as it came. "It's weird," she said, though from the pinched concern on her face, "weird" was a weak term for what she felt. "Why can't I get through to Tallah?" I felt her panic and kicked myself for not sharing my worries about Mom's probable course of action.

I quickly explained what I assumed was true while Gram nodded and Sassafras snorted his agreement. Shenka visibly relaxed, though her forehead creased in anger when I finished.

"Would it not be better to share this will all covens?" I'd never heard such an edge in her voice. Winced. Felt terrible she'd spent the last three days fearing the Hensley's were gone, too.

And since she just repeated what I'd been thinking, I shrugged. "There's no way anyone else has been attacked." I had to believe Mom would have told us if another incident occurred. Okay, maybe not. But Quaid would have. "But if she has kept it secret, it explains why the other covens haven't reached out to us." Not like they would anyway. Bunch of secretive biddies minding their own business so much the world could fall apart and they wouldn't realize it until it was too late. "I think we should both go check on our people."

Gram nabbed my plate and helped herself to my dinner as I stood with Shenka.

"Keep an eye on the place," I said, feeling far too much joy considering the circumstances. But I was about to do something. And acting felt like the closest thing to happiness I had access to right now.

Gram waved us off with her fork, not looking up as Shenka and I, Charlotte on our heels, left the kitchen and went out the back door.

"Be careful." Sassafras followed us, pausing at the threshold. "I'll stay with Ethpeal and keep an eye on things. But you two, don't do anything stupid." He hesitated. "On the other hand, maybe I should go with you."

I let the door close in his face. "Stay put," I said. "Gram might need you."

He swatted at the screen, but didn't comment as we crossed the lawn, heading for the park.

"You realize this could possibly get us arrested?" I glanced sideways at Shenka as I spoke.

She turned to me as we crossed the wards, eyes wide, face innocent. "But we're just making sure our people are okay."

Snort. "Perfect," I said. "If Mom blows it, you handle her." Because if I had to plaster that face on, I'd fail.

New wards sat in place at the Dumonts, but only around the front door. The veil deposited us on the wide, stone steps, and I didn't hesitate to enter without knocking. Not like anyone in the family would have answered. The place felt like a tomb. Three Enforcers swooped down, but stopped when I let them feel my power.

"Just here to check on our people." Okay, so I could lie, too. Just not to Mom.

The one in the lead, a hefty woman with huge hands and a flat face hesitated. They must have had conflicting orders because, after a moment, she shrugged and backed off.

I led Shenka through the house, up the stairs toward Mia's room with a level of confidence I didn't feel, knowing I was going against Mom's orders, but unable to just sit on my hands any longer.

What was that woman doing?

Mia's door creaked as I let us in, the heavy wood swinging wide. Mia sat propped up on her countless pillows, purple and black velvet holding her up. She didn't seem to see us, staring off into space while a slender woman with Dumont features hovered at her side, head down, blonde hair hanging limp. She at least looked up as we came closer, blue eyes full of tears.

"Coven Leader." The young woman, about my age I guessed, snuffled and wiped her nose on her sleeve. Her faint French accent confirmed her breeding. "I don't know what to do to help her." She gestured vaguely at Mia who continued to stare into space.

Shenka acted before I could as my discomfort grew,

my second sitting next to the Dumont girl.

"I'm Sashenka Hensley," she said. "What's your name?"

"Marie," the girl said. Sniffed again. "Marie Dumont. I'm Mia's second cousin." My power brushed over her, felt how weak she was. Did whoever stole the Dumont power take personal magic as well or was the Dumont family really so fragile?

Nothing would surprise me, Gram snapped in my mind. *Leave Shenka with the girls and go poke around already.*

Bossy. Fine.

I slipped from the room to the sound of Shenka comforting Marie, Charlotte trailing behind, nose upturned. I heard her sniff a few times and raised an eyebrow at her, but she just shook her head.

"Rupe," she said. "But the rest of the scents are too muddled to make out."

Surely the Enforcers tested for power in the same way Charlotte's nose tested for scent. I let my energy slide outwards, thin little threads, staying low and almost undetectable—I hoped. If the Enforcers caught me snooping, I'd be in major trouble.

Like this. Gram seized my magic and spun it around, turning it inside out, so the power reflected back on itself. Super simple, absolutely easy.

Why didn't I think of it?

Enforcer trick, Gram grunted. *Get to it.*

Promising myself I'd turn over whatever I found to Mom and Pender immediately, I snuck down the corridor, letting my newly disguised magic wander the halls and rooms and multi-floors of the castle while Charlotte opened her nose and tried to unravel the mess of smells. I was so focused on trying to find the source of the attack, I totally missed the fact I wasn't alone anymore until I almost stumbled on the three witches, huddled close, whispering to each other.

It was only Charlotte's rumbling growl of warning that kept me from barging right into them. I stumbled to a halt, looking around the vast library just before I met a pair of chill blue eyes now locked on me. Andre Dumont straightened, falling silent, his two sons equally still. Gone was the harsh arrogance I was used to, the sharp jab of superiority the Dumont men carried around with them. Instead, Andre's attempt to appear better-than fell sadly short, a play in petulance echoed by Jean Marc and Kristophe.

They were the last people I'd expected to run into. I guess I privately hoped maybe they were among the dead.

Bad, Syd. Bad, bad.

"Come to gloat?" Andre's deep, rich voice sounded hollow in the vast room full of books with its arching ceiling. Odette's only son's accent was stronger than I remembered, perhaps influenced by the turn of events.

I shrugged. "Just checking on my people." Fell flat.

Yup. Oh well, not like I was really going to fool anyone.

Jean Marc glared, his short, dark hair normally neat now a mess while Kristophe's attempt at a model pose, his favorite, just came across as sad. Desperately sad.

"I haven't seen you since Mom's trial." Andre had been in the thick of things when it came to Mom's arrest, I knew it. Absolutely in Odette's confidence. But his claim he'd been coerced by his own mother was accepted by the Council and he'd been set free. No longer the Dumont's representative on Council, he'd retreated in defeat to the Dumont family. To hide, for all I knew. Now the only direct living descendant aside from Mia, this had to be hitting him almost as hard. If for different and more selfish reasons.

How the mighty—in his own mind—had fallen.

Andre's gaze flickered over my shoulder, a tight smile pulling at his mouth, bitterness rampant. "*Bonjour*, Charlotte," he said. "We've missed you, *cher*."

She chuffed softly, but didn't comment, though I felt the wolf in her stir in fury. She'd been Andre's possession for years, her whole pack had. The Sidhe hound Galleytrot freed her, freed all of them, but she still hadn't located her father, Raoul. At least, as far as I knew. The way Charlotte kept to herself, he could have been sleeping at the foot of her bed and I probably wouldn't have known.

"I'm sorry about what happened." I surprised myself

with how genuine my words came out. So much all three Dumonts flinched.

Andre bowed his head just a fraction. "Your immediate assistance when summoned was greatly appreciated." Man, that had to hurt. Gram cackled in my head, still eavesdropping, but I wasn't about to give her the boot. She deserved the chance to see the Dumont family thanking me. Made her day, I bet.

My eyes drifted to Kristophe's right hand as it twitched, a white stone turning in his fingers as I answered. "I was asked to help," I said, something stirring in my chest, crackling. "And I didn't hesitate." What was it? Poking me, prodding at me to pay attention.

More than they would have done for us, Gram snarled.

As I examined the feeling, the walls around the idea split, burst into a dark bubble building inside my stomach as I stared at the stone in Kristophe's hand. He clenched his fist around it when he noticed me watching, but that just made my anxiety grow.

No. It couldn't be. But it made the most logical sense, didn't it?

Didn't it?

"Give that to me." I held out my hand, the demand backed with power. Kristophe refused at first before Andre snarled at him in French. Long hair hanging over his shoulder, Kristophe shrugged delicately before dropping the white stone into my palm even as my entire body stilled.

Fear like I'd never know zinged through me as I reached for the stone.

And felt nothing.

Not crystal. Not a trap for power after all. Just a smooth, white stone.

I handed it back with my fear still alive, kicking myself I hadn't even considered what I now assumed had to be the truth. The blossom of understanding felt like an epiphany, one I should have had the moment I felt the attack on Mia. Even without proof, what other explanation could there be?

It had to be them.

The Brotherhood.

Oh. My. Swearword.

Gram swore in my head so loudly I almost jumped. *We're all idiots*, she snarled. *Get back here right now.*

I spun from the three Dumonts, knowing I'd likely made a very terrible mistake, letting three days pass. Three days for the Brotherhood to track and plot another coven's demise. To take another family's magic.

Desperation clenched a fist around my lungs, my heart as I thought of Shenka's sister on the West coast. Of how I could have been wrong, after all. Didn't trust Mom to keep me posted, feared Quaid was under orders to stay silent.

Tallah. The Hensleys. All of the covens.

Please, please. No.

I was almost back to Mia's room, reaching for Shenka when I heard the first scream.

chapter ten

Panic drove me through the door, power gathered, expecting a battle with sorcery, the Brotherhood, someone dying.

Enforcers flooded the doorway behind me, shoving me forward, gaping at Mia. Who stood, mouth wide open, on her bed. Screaming. Screaming, as if she were being murdered, at the top of her lungs. Even the Enforcers screeched to a halt and stared while Mia had a very ugly, very emotional breakdown.

"I WANT IT BACK!" Her wailing words drove spikes through my ears, the pain behind them almost as bad as the volume she used. No one had to ask her what "it" was. The blank absence of the family magic gaped like an open wound. I glanced toward Shenka who crouched on the floor, shielding Marie who sobbed, blood running from her nose. Whatever triggered Mia's eruption injured the young Dumont.

She's out of control. I sent that tight beam to the Enforcer beside me, the same woman I'd encountered at the front door. *Do something.*

I'm not allowed to interfere. The woman's equally tight reply came through as though she mentally clenched her teeth.

She had to be kidding me. *Fine*, I snapped back. *Stay out of the way.*

Magic surging, I stepped forward and reached for Mia, spinning power around her, cutting off her desperate yearning, tying her down with blue flames. She collapsed into the magic, but her rage didn't dissipate. Instead, she refocused it.

Guess where?

"GET OUT!" Her feeble energy battered against me like a butterfly trying to escape a glass jar. "AND TAKE YOUR WITCHES WITH YOU!"

And that was that. The Enforcer lieutenant shrugged at me, brow furrowed, mental voice apologetic as she spoke. *You heard her*, she sent. *Time to go, Leader Hayle.*

Damn it.

Damn it.

The twins appeared as if by magic—no kidding—the rest of my family joining her as I clomped my way down the wide stairs, fury waging war with guilt and disappointment while Mia's shrieking chased me all the way from her bedroom. The two Enforcer escorts didn't give me a chance to do much but head for the exit.

And honestly? At that point, it felt a lot like good riddance. Especially if I was right about the Brotherhood. If the sorcerer league hell-bent on destroying all magic but their own really was behind the theft of the Dumont power, I had my own troubles to consider. And Mia's family wasn't part of them.

Finally, Gram sent.

I almost missed him, the familiar pale, scarred face, white hair, diminutive body hiding behind a doorway. But his open smile and bright blue eyes stood out like a sore thumb in this house of pain and loss. When he waved at me, I nodded ever so slightly back. That seemed to be enough. He vanished as I passed out the front door of the Dumont mansion, hearing it boom shut behind me.

It wasn't until I delivered my people home again and walked into the kitchen with my entire body clenched to keep from flying apart I was able to formulate the words I needed.

"Why was Demetrius Strong at the Dumont mansion?" The former head of the Chosen of the Light tried several times to kill me before becoming an ally. Of sorts. If an insane sorcerer could be considered an ally.

Gram stood at the kitchen window, one foot tapping the floor, soundless in her fuzzy sock. When she turned to face me, her pinched expression told me she'd been as deep in her own thoughts as I had been in mine.

"Gram," I said while Shenka stepped aside, arms wrapped around herself. "You knew him before, when you were an Enforcer." She admitted as much, or gave me that impression, when Demetrius helped me against the vampire queens. "Who is he working for?"

Gram shrugged, a sharp, angry gesture. "I don't know," she said. "But if he's here, you can damned well believe we missed the obvious." One of her thin, wrinkled hands slammed down on the counter. "How did we miss it? How did we fail to realize the Brotherhood was the logical choice?"

I shuddered and turned from her, head down, hating to say what I did next. "Maybe because they wanted us to." Gram spun on me as though I'd slapped her even as I looked up and met her eyes, feeling a dullness rise inside me. "You know they've done it before. They're subtle enough at it, we'd never know."

Gram shook her head, white hair flying, rage striking sparks in her eyes. "No," she snapped. "No. I don't believe it." She stomped one foot, the floor shaking as her power expelled through the sole of her foot. "Absolutely not."

Well, if she was that sure... "Then why?"

Gram's scowl was so deep my face hurt in sympathy. "Because," she said. "We've been complacent. Too wrapped up in the loss of the power, in the tragedy, to think straight. Told to stay the hell out of it, weren't we?" She began to pace. "So no, not the Brotherhood, girl. They didn't put that suggestion in our heads." Gram stopped, faced me, the woman she was, the Enforcer who had been, showing in her eyes. "No, that was left by someone much closer to home."

I gasped as I made the connection. "You think Mom...?"

Gram spun so her back was to me, hands gripping the counter edge, gaze locked outside. "Miriam."

"But why?" Shenka spoke when I couldn't. Not while bile rose in my throat, my stomach churning, mix of rage and disbelief stabbing me so hard I almost threw up. "Why would Miriam use suggestion on us?"

"Only one answer to that," Gram said. "She already knew it was the Brotherhood and needed to protect Syd."

Oh no, she did *not*. "I'm going to kill her." It was the only logical next step. Murdering my mother. Absolutely.

Gram kicked the lower cupboards twice before turning again, pinning me with her faded blue eyes. "Me first," she said.

Shenka stepped between us as the plan formed and grew in our minds, the perfect plan to dispose of Mom's body when we were done. "She had her reasons," my second said in a voice meant to soothe. "Clearly she never expected Syd to try to investigate."

She knew me better than that. Which is why she used

the suggestion. And it had to have cost her, considering it held for three days. Three wasted days.

She'd suffer. Oh, how she'd suffer.

Gram grunted, shoulders sagging. "It was a terrible decision," she said, voice falling to a whisper, "but I understand her motives. Might have done the same thing." Her eyes met mine again as I spluttered. "To save the family."

Those four words were a splash of cold water. Mom warned me, didn't she? And since when did I ever listen? Didn't give her the right to take matters into her own hands and I'd absolutely make sure she understood so in crystal clarity. But the family.

The family.

"I need to talk to her." Preferably after I'd cooled off a bit, but there was no helping my state of mind, not now. Not after I'd wasted three freaking days.

"What about Demetrius?" Shenka looked back and forth between us. She'd been filled in on everything and though she'd not met him, she understood how important he could be.

"I don't know," I said. "He used to lead the Chosen. Then he was working for Batsheva." I clenched my jaw against the memory of her fangs in my neck, comforted by the fact her shell grew mold in my basement. "He might be working for the Brotherhood now." Though Liander Belaisle, the Brotherhood leader I'd met when

Trill and Owen Zornov first came into my life, treated Demetrius with nothing but disdain the last time they met one another.

And Demetrius swore to me he was on my side. The fact he showed himself gave me some comfort.

Some.

"Demetrius Strong had older masters even than the Brotherhood," Gram said, grim faced, but with a spark of hope in her voice. "The Steam Union recruited him long ago."

The what?

Gram must have known I'd just ply her with endless questions. For once, she gave up what she knew without a fight.

"There are two camps," she said. "The Brotherhood and the Steam Union. Both sects of sorcerers. Only one sect is out for magical domination. And the other wants to find a way we can all work together."

I snorted. Couldn't help it. The idea of good sorcerers made me want to puke all over again.

Gram pinned me with her gaze. "There are two sides to everything, girl," she said. "Don't ever forget it."

Fine. Whatever. "I'm going to see Mom," I said. "If Demetrius has something to share, he knows how to find us." I couldn't worry about him right now.

"Perfect," Gram said, linking her arm with mine, eyes glittering anger. "I'm coming with you."

A tiny, infinitesimal part of me actually felt sorry for Mom.

The rest of me still hadn't decided if she'd survive the encounter or not.

CHAPTER ELEVEN

We found her in her office, bent over a stack of paperwork. Didn't bother knocking. Or using regular channels. I was in a bad enough mood over the whole mess I simply slid us through the edge of the wards. The pentagram necklace I wore around my neck carried enough of Mom's essence to fool the shielding around her office into letting us through while the touch of Gram's Enforcer power, what she still carried with her, sealed the deal.

To Mom's credit, she didn't freak out. Just looked up with a resigned expression, blue eyes snapping fire as she waved at her door, sealing it with a rush of magic.

"I've been waiting for you," she said. "Hungry?"

Her attitude knocked me totally off guard. I'd lunged into the veil expecting a fight, ready for one. Couldn't wait. But, instead of our usual nuclear party-time, Mom rose from her desk and gestured at the small table beside the window. The scent of roasted chicken and veggies preceded the magical arrival of dinner, making my stomach growl and mouth water.

So not fair.

Charlotte remained by the door, eyes never leaving us as Gram sat with a cackle of delight, tearing the chicken apart with her bare hands, slapping a slab of torn white meat on my plate and a leg and wing on her own before she licked both of her hands clean.

Well, at least she did the licking after she served me.

Mom didn't flinch, sitting with a sigh, her knife and fork carving some of her own selection before she helped herself to carrots and a small stack of mashed potatoes. Gram shoveled a large dollop next to my chicken, followed by a ladle full of veggies while I crossed my arms over my chest and glared at my mother.

"You coerced me." This whole little show of hers, dinner, calm, yeah. Not buying it. And while I had to admit the edge was gone from my anger, my demon's bubbling rage could bring it back anytime.

Mom met my eyes as Gram poured gravy over my potatoes, smothering my chicken in the hot, fragrant liquid.

"I did," she said. Took a bite of chicken, eyes never leaving mine.

Damn her. How could I keep my temper up when

she didn't fight back?

"Girl." Gram prodded me with one sharp index finger. "Eat."

Like I could think of food at a time like this. I halfheartedly chewed a mouthful, hating how delicious it was, even as Mom took a sip of water, dabbing at the corner of her mouth with her napkin.

"It was necessary," she said. "There's more going on than you realize. I had to protect you, Syd."

"No," I shot back, fork rattling against the side of my plate as I tossed it down. Ah, there was my anger. Right on cue. "You needed to trust me, Mom. But, as usual, you tried to keep me in the dark. Left me to find out things on my own."

"You went to see the Dumonts." Mom's expression didn't waver, still cool and collected, though the barb in her voice told me we were going to have a fight after all.

"The Brotherhood is behind this." Gram's words cut the air between Mom and me, jerking our attention from each other to my grandmother. She stuffed a large mouthful of chicken, veggies and potato into her mouth, a drip of gravy running down her chin as she chewed with great enthusiasm.

Mom cleared her throat, nodded. "They could be," she said. "We think."

"We know." The one bite of dinner I'd taken curdled in my stomach. "Demetrius Strong was at the Dumont mansion."

Mom's blue eyes flashed, one arched eyebrow rising. "What did he tell you?"

Oh, so she could keep things from me, but I was supposed to give up the secret recipe? Yeah, not happening. Sucked he didn't tell me anything. Would have been nice to have something to hang over her. Instead, I turned my face away, glaring over the top of her desk at the portrait of her hanging on the wall. Giant. Bigger than life.

Made me want to set the stupid thing on fire.

"Doesn't matter now," Gram said, belching softly into one fist before swilling down a large gulp of water. "None of it does." She stared at Mom a moment, then aimed her faded blue eyes at me. Power shone in her face, grim expression pushing against me as much as her magic. "If we've learned nothing, it's that we all have to work together."

Mom nodded slowly, sighing as she sat back, tossing her napkin to the table. "I know," she said. "But there are certain things Syd must stay out of. For the safety of the coven."

I'd heard that before. Pissed me off how true it was. "So, the Brotherhood." I reined in my temper, my demon snorting and snuffling as I shoved her down. "Not Ameline after all." But there was Rupe... Ameline had to have inside information.

Mom's right hand twitched, fingers tapping the table top. "She refuses to talk," Mom said. "Not even under Enforcer coercion."

Gram grunted. "They aren't pushing hard enough."

I had no doubt Gram wouldn't have the same trouble, but Mom shook her head, face relaxing as she rubbed her eyes with her fingertips.

"It's not that simple," she said. Looked up and met my eyes, hers full of sadness and fear. "She's managed to find a way to protect herself."

From the way Mom flinched, I knew I wasn't going to like what she had to say next.

"We originally thought she lost access to the powers she stole after they were removed," Mom said. "We now know that's not the case."

Um, what? "Todd is fine." I had just seen the young Happern yesterday playing with his sister. Ameline's theft of his soul and the subsequent return of it thanks to yours truly didn't seem to have done him any damage. Our demon family settled in quite nicely with the coven and seemed more than content. And from what I'd seen of Liam and his Sidhe soul, Cian, everything was fine there, too. Shaylee murmured her agreement, a quick check over of herself reaffirming what I already knew.

We were fine. All intact.

So what was Mom talking about?

Gram sighed out a breath, eyes narrowing. "She

opened new pathways."

Mom nodded. "We didn't know until it was too late."

"Pathways?" I looked back and forth between them, pressure building inside me. "What are you talking about?"

Mom's hand stilled at last. "Ameline never intended to keep the power she stole," she said. "But she needed enough strength from the souls she took to burn open the pathways to those powers." Mom's fingers started up again. "She created new spaces inside herself, literally recreated herself."

Gram whistled, shook her head. "No matter how much we hate that girl," she said, "she's got guts."

My brain churned, trying to assimilate what Mom said. "She's made herself a demon." That was impossible, wasn't it?

Mom took another sip of water before answering. "And a vampire," she said. "And a Sidhe."

No way. Hang on a second. "How did she manage the Sidhe thing?" I reached for Shaylee again as my princess rebelled at the idea. She was whole. "She doesn't have a Sidhe soul."

Mom's jaw clenched, eyes dropping to her plate. "We believe the reason she wanted multiple Sidhe souls inside her had nothing to do with keeping them." When she finally looked up, her discomfort made me want to squirm. "However she managed it, Ameline now carries the soul of an infant Sidhe inside her. Brand new and growing rapidly."

Oh. My. Swearword.

Gross.

Just. Freaking.

Holy.

Shaylee lost it inside me, thrashing, fury raging, a film of power flaring over my vision, tinting everything before me green. "She got Shaylee pregnant?" With Cian?

Gram gaped at me before chuckling. "You wanted that boy for yourself," she said. "What's the big deal?"

Oh, this was a very big deal, thank you very much. Huge. Massive.

Shaylee shuddered, retreated, but not before Mom shook her head.

"We believe it was Cian and the queen's aide, Bronagh, who created the infant soul," Mom said.

Shaylee shuddered, calmed a little, though I could still feel her fury churning, joined with the anger of my demon. Even my vampire hissed her unhappiness, usual stoic quiet shattered at the thought of Shaylee being used.

"How do you know?" I slammed my chair back, lurching to my feet. I had to investigate. To be sure. Mom rose herself, power sliding around me, holding me still.

Oh no, she did *not*.

"We've had her tested," Mom said. Firmly. Very firmly.

"You're not Sidhe," I snarled.

"No," she said. "But Liam is."

Liam...

"I had to keep you out of it." Mom wrung her hands, face twisting in a mix of anxiety and grief. "I had no choice, Syd."

I shook off her power with a burst of demon fire, entire body going cold as my flaring temper faded to absolute icy fury. At her. At the guy who was supposed to love me.

Double betrayal.

"So now Ameline has all the power she needs," I said, words frozen daggers, slicing through Mom's defenses. "And thanks to the Council, she's been letting her magic grow over all these months while you try to figure out how to pull your fingers out of your butts and strip her magic." A hitching pressure squeezed my chest, the need to destroy something rising. "What the hell are you waiting for?"

Mom's own anger crackled suddenly, her worry turning to aggression. "I'm doing the best I can," she snapped. "My job, Syd. And as much as you clearly don't trust me to do what I have to, I have limited options."

Gram rose to her feet, fluffy socks silent on the floor. She stood between us, a wall of calm holding us apart. "That girl can't be allowed to grow any further," Gram said in the most reasonable tone I'd ever heard from her.

"You know that, Miriam. If she has access to sorcery as well, which I have no doubt is the case, you have a baby maji on your hands."

Mom shuddered, visibly pulling herself under control as my skin goosebumped, rage washing away in a surge of fear.

"How do you think she's been able to keep us from breaking her?" Mom turned away, arms around herself, staring out the window. "Even as weak as she is, our power is no match for creation energy."

What an absolute disaster.

"Then let me do it." Gladly, with bells on, singing hallelujah in a pink tutu. "She might have maji power, but I'm stronger than her." All of my alter egos surged in answer.

Mom flinched. "We can't," she said. "We must follow the law. Ameline Benoit has to stand trial."

My teeth made a grinding noise as I fought my need to swear at her. "When, then?"

"The Enforcers are still gathering evidence." Mom dropped her arms, shoulders slumping forward. "It could take a few more months."

What were they doing, creating evidence? "Mom, you have more than enough to take her to trial."

She turned to me, eyes sad. "I know," she said. "But the law dictates we must be thorough, Syd. And Ameline's activities go well beyond her encounters with you and the Hayle coven."

Fingers in more rotten pies? Why didn't that surprise me?

"There's one way around this," I said. "Let me talk to her. Two minutes. I'll shut her down, at least. Seal off her new powers." Mom had to know if Ameline was allowed to continue to nurture her newborn maji ability, things would only end in disaster.

Gram answered before Mom could. "You can't," she said, voice grim.

She said what?

"She's been badgering me to visit her since she was captured," I said.

"I know," Mom said, shoulders going back, face returning to a mask of calm, clearly triggered by Gram's unhappy support. "But regardless, you aren't permitted to see her. Even if you weren't one of her main accusers, Ameline is being held in our most protected prison and isn't allowed visitors."

chapter twelve

I spent the next two heartbeats looking back and forth between my mother and my grandmother, mouth opening and closing as I tried to comprehend the stupidest thing I'd heard in my entire life.

"What the hell is wrong with you?" Okay, I didn't mean to jump on Mom like that, I really didn't. But it came out, boy did it ever, in absolute shock.

I could have been more tactful, I know that now. But I really think, no matter how I called her an idiot, Mom's reaction would have been the same.

The tell-tale mask of cold rose, her whole body rigid.

Yup, went too far this time, Syd.

Every time.

"Dinner is over." Mom swept from the table, returning to her desk, back to us. "Return to your family, Coven Leader, and leave this matter to me."

I hated it—hated it so much—when she pulled the Council Leader bullcrap on me. My mind reached out for hers, to connect. Met empty blankness.

Before blue fire crackled over my mind and sent me staggering back with a cry of pain.

"How dare you?" Mom strode forward, flames rippling around her, the power of her office raging as she towered over me where I bent in half, my hands pressed to my temples. I heard the growl of Charlotte's wolf, dimly registered her yip of hurt.

Tell me she didn't just attack Charlotte, too. Oh *hell* no. I wasn't taking that from her, no way, no how. My own magic answered, all the power at my command rising in a wave of fury as I straightened to face the woman before me, ready to fight.

Charlotte crouched beside me, blue power crackling over her as she twitched and whined, the wolf in her fighting to escape while Mom's magic flared, blue eyes full of rage. I severed the attack with power of my own, felt the wards in the room spring to life, ready to come for me if I acted again, knew without a doubt this place was coming down and I couldn't wait to tear it apart with my bare hands.

No one hurt Charlotte. No one.

Gram's hand pressed to my chest, sliding through the sparking energy surrounding me while her other fisted, tapping against Mom's shoulder. Something snapped inside me, sending me backward again, this time with horror growing in my gut, the knowledge I would have attacked my own mother given another moment.

And that she'd already attacked me.

Mom's face twisted, tears rising in her eyes, her magic retreating, one hand rising toward me.

"Syd," she whispered, before turning to Charlotte, hand over her mouth in horror. "I'm so sorry."

No way. Not now. Maybe later.

Maybe.

"Let's go, girl," Gram said, taking my elbow, leading me to the door, my bodywere firmly gripped in her other hand. The wards around the exit flared and fell as Mom broke them to allow us to leave. I refused to look back, my heart thudding in my chest, pain like I'd never known driving spikes through my chest while Charlotte snarled over her shoulder before thudding the door firmly shut behind her.

I collapsed against a chair as the door closed behind me, clutching at my throat while the agony rose. Pain ripped through me, my heart stuttering a few beats. Had Mom done some damage I missed, her power still coming for me?

Gram pulled me to her, power sliding over me, supporting me as I realized the hurt I felt wasn't physical.

I don't know why it hit me so hard just then, the fact my own mother struck at me with her magic, treated me like an enemy. No matter what happened, she'd always managed to see past her anger and admit I was right.

That I'd done what I had to do.

Not this time. My mother just attacked me for trying to reach out to her. And now my heart wanted to die.

I gasped for air, unable to focus, shoving away from Gram, staggering through the sitting room in Mom's quarters, not seeing the dark wood walls, the glaring eyes of the portraits of other Leaders. Not caring that Mom's hideous little secretary, Maurice, glared as he huffed past, an arrogant sneer on his face. I made it to the hall, the elevators, fell inside one, barely catching myself as I grasped the hand rail and clutched it like a life line as the sobs threatening to tear me in two finally escaped.

I'd survived so much over the years since Batsheva Moromond and her evil husband tried to take over my family. Through pain and loss and heartache, I'd always had Mom to lean on, in the end. Even when I didn't think it was true, she had my back, did her best, even when I lost it.

But she'd never, not in our darkest moments, ever struck me with magic. The dull memory of her hand on my cheek reminded me of the one and only blow she'd delivered, so long ago I barely remembered being sixteen and a pain in the ass.

This. This was so different that slap didn't even qualify in the same category.

Gram's hand settled on my back, rubbed small circles while I choked on my tears, on my disbelief, more shaken than really damaged. I turned to her, hugged her, trembling so violently I thought I might fall. Gram held me up, slim body stronger than I'd given her credit for, cheek pressed to my hair as she rocked me gently.

Girl, she sent. *I know. And if I could save you from this, I would.*

I couldn't form a coherent thought, not yet.

Listen to me, she sent. *Your mother... the pressure of her job, of keeping you safe... I'm not making excuses.* Her anger flared, settled. *And turning on you was inexcusable. But you have to pull yourself together.*

I didn't want to hear it, hear her. No matter what happened, what mess I was in, Mom never, ever lashed out at me like that.

Heartbreaking.

Sydlynn. Gram's voice cut through my grief. *Enough.*

I snuffled, pulled back from her, feeling like the support system of my entire life just shattered under me and left me to dangle over a chasm of darkness.

The elevator dinged, the doors opening to the bottom floor. Gram guided me out, past a pair of startled looking witches who dodged the still furious and hyper-protective Charlotte, my grandmother's arm linked through mine as I wiped at my cheeks with my sleeve, the fragments of my soul weeping and raging in alternating surges, my alter egos fighting for balance.

Gram planted me on a bench, Charlotte hovering, vibrating with rage, behind me. My grandmother held my hands while I vented the last of my emotions. By the time I was done, tears dried, mind and body numb, hands still shaking, my anger had won.

"There's something wrong with Mom." I couldn't bring myself to believe she'd acted of her own free will. She had to be under some kind of control, coercion...

Gram watched, silent and grim until I finally had to look away.

There was nothing wrong with Mom. Except I'd finally pushed her past the point of no return.

"Are you done?" There wasn't any judgment in Gram's question, but I felt her impatience and shrugged.

"Whatever," I said, rising to my feet, turning my back on Massachusetts Hall and my mother. No more running to her when things went wrong. No more keeping her informed, Council Leader or not. She made it clear I was no longer welcome.

Mom and I were through.

I met Charlotte's eyes, felt her barely contained rage. Reached for her with my magic, felt the pain in her, that Mom hurt her after all. Healed what I could with my spirit magic, my vampire whispering softly to me, whispers I ignored as Charlotte's skin, once covered in a pattern of dark red burns healed to normal pale tan.

Unbelievable. And unacceptable.

I had to get the hell out of here before my anger drove me back into Mom's office to finish what she started.

Gram's arm slid through mine again. Before I could slice open the veil to take us home, she turned us and steered me toward the other side of campus.

We're not going home just yet, Gram sent. *That is, if you're still willing to break a few of your mother's precious rules?*

Since when had rules stopped me? I frowned at her as my feet followed, carrying me along, my bodywere pacing behind us.

Where are we going? I firmly stuffed Mom's betrayal to the back of my mind. I'd dig it out later, dissect it, rage and weep over it some more before smothering it in chocolate.

Coping mechanisms rocked.

If we get caught, Gram sent, *this was your idea.* She cackled a moment before falling silent. *I'm serious, girl. We'll both be arrested and they won't even make keys for our cells. If we get cells. More like bottomless pits.*

Warning received. Recklessness roused. *I'm in*, I sent.

Gram paused, turned to me, a frown creasing her wrinkled brow. *I really should go alone*, she sent. *But you're the only one who can get us the information we desperately need.*

Where are we going, exactly? I kept moving as she began her tromping way again, glad for the distraction, for something to focus on besides my flaring anger as the peak of Memorial Chapel came into view.

To see Ameline, of course, Gram sent.

A black blot in my soul rejoiced.

The perfect revenge against my mother. I'd take it.

chapter thirteen

Gram finally pulled me to a halt in front of the bench next to the chapel. I knew this bench, spent a very uncomfortable few minutes fighting off my former bestie here during my first week at Harvard. Alison's ghost attacked me, wanting the vampire essence now living inside me. Guilt rose, as it always did when I thought of Alison. Tracking down the now tainted echo of who Alison Morgan had been wasn't on the top of my priority list, despite the fact my vampire worried the portions of her essence Alison stole turned the former cheergirl into some kind of vampire/ghost hybrid. I'd kept my ears and eyes open, but hadn't heard a whisper about Alison since the night the Star Club fell apart. The night Alison first tasted blood.

A shudder ran through me as Gram spun and pointed a sharp index finger my way. "You two stay close," she said. I caught Charlotte's sharp nod beside me and briefly considered trying to send her home. Like that was going to happen. My bodywere's wolf eyes met my gaze, no sign of calm and unassuming remaining.

Yeah. Charlotte was coming with us.

Okay, then.

Gram turned toward the bench and made a soft sound, kind of like she trilled the beginning of a song. Her hands came together in a sharp jerk, power sparking between them before she slowly drew them apart. The hair on my arms stood up as Enforcer magic bounced back from her. I quickly shielded what she was doing before anyone could react to it.

Gram didn't seem too concerned, all of her focus on the gap forming between her hands. The line of blue magic parted in the middle, a window into somewhere else shimmering to life. Turned out I wasn't the only one who could open a veil. Though this one felt nothing like the rubbery membrane I used to travel, the wall between my plane and Demonicon. It buzzed with life, humming back to Gram, welcoming her.

A stone hallway appeared as she drew her fingers apart, a slice through the veil as tall as she was vibrating around the edges, blue fire licking at her hands to match the border of the tear. By the time she was done, her song ended, a large opening in the fabric of this plane led to what amounted to a castle corridor on the other side.

"This entrance isn't used very often," Gram said, turning to meet my eyes. Sweat beaded on her upper lip as her chin trembled from the strain, though from the sparkle in her gaze she was having the time of her life. "So we should be fine. Now, everybody in."

Charlotte didn't hesitate, pushing past me, nose in the air, snuffling as she stepped through. I followed behind her, staying close, feeling the subtle sting of the veil brush against my hand as I touched the edge of the hole Gram made. She hissed behind me, practically pushing against my back until we all stood in the corridor, leaving the warmth of the sun for the dim coolness of the stone hall.

I turned just in time to see Gram bring her hands together again, the tear sealing shut with a slurping sound reminding me of something being swallowed. Gram panted, hands shaking as she grinned at me.

"Haven't done that in a while," she said with a broad wink. "Forgot how much fun it was."

Fun. Right.

I looked around, the scent of damp stone and distant wood smoke reaching my nose, the air chill with moisture. A blank wall stood where we'd come through, square stones sealed with dark mortar climbing well over our heads. A small window at least eight feet up showing only a dark and gloomy sky. Gram's hands reached into the air, small flashes of blue preceding the appearance of three black robes as she snatched them from nothing before tossing them to me and Charlotte. Her own draped across her thin shoulders, black hood coming up over her halo of white hair.

As if some kind of weird switch had been flipped, all of a sudden Gram looked like an Enforcer. Her spine straightened, a youthful vitality coming over her face as she did a happy tap dance on the stones under her feet, only the fuzzy socks she wore visible and giving away the fact she wasn't really one of the order anymore.

Or was she?

Her fingers brushed over my cheek, a tingle of magic passing between us as a foreign power integrated into my personal shielding. I recognized her touch immediately, but this was distilled, raw, as wild as any earth magic I'd felt from Galleytrot and his master of the Sidhe hunt.

Gram touched Charlotte too, before shuddering like a dog shedding water.

"Enforcer power," Gram said, voice deeper, steadier than usual. Without the edge of crazy I was used to. "It won't hold up under careful scrutiny, but I don't think anyone will bother us. No outsider has ever made it this far, so they have no reason to wonder. Or ask questions." She glared at me, one finger jabbing my chest. "Head down, follow close, and shut the hell up. Got it?"

I nodded even as my stomach fell to my feet, dread as heavy as the velvet folds of the stolen cloak I wore.

This was very bad. But I'd agreed to it, hadn't I?

Impersonating an Enforcer. A new low, Syd.

But the joy in Gram's face, the way she turned from me and strode off with eager steps, stilled my bout of nerves. She wouldn't have brought us here if she didn't think it was important. And I agreed with her. Ameline had information I needed, information Mom already admitted the criminal witch would only give to me. Adopting her confident stride if not her attitude, I went after her, Charlotte trailing behind me.

"So where are we?" We'd passed through the veil, but this place wasn't familiar and I began to wonder just how many alternate planes there were. Considering the demon plane was a combination of hundreds of smaller ones bonded together, the possibilities really boggled.

"Nowhere special," Gram said with amusement in her voice. "Just a little place we like to call home." She paused. "They, I mean."

"Who they?" Though from the robes we all wore, I was beginning to understand why Quaid was so hard to find, why he seemed to disappear at times. Understanding dawned as Gram spoke.

"Welcome to the Enforcer stronghold," she said. "Training ground, quarters. Home of the High Council prison."

Prison?

Gulp.

Right. Ameline. Still. The word sent shivers through

me as I walked behind my grandmother, just hoping this sneak visit wasn't a sign I'd find myself a more permanent resident in the future.

Wasn't holding my breath.

Chapter Fourteen

The stronghold seemed to be a maze of endless stone corridors, punctuated by the occasional giant room with towering ceilings. Everything was arched, fitted columns sweeping overhead, reminding me of a medieval cathedral. What few windows we encountered showed a barren landscape, the sky that same dark cloud cover I'd first seen, uniform and dull, as bleak as the browned earth, empty and flat of vegetation or anything else living for what looked like miles.

The stronghold itself felt endless, engulfing us as we walked, the vastness making me hunch my shoulders, tiny and inconsequential. What were we doing again? And why did I care so much? A heavy apathy rode my back, slowing me down until only prodding from Charlotte behind me kept me moving.

Gram finally turned to find we'd fallen behind and

frowned. Her fingers touched my cheek again, Enforcer magic sparking my own power.

"Sorry," Gram said. "I forgot about the warding. Any normal magic user would be weeping on her knees by now."

I glanced at Charlotte, caught the tightness of her jaw, the way her lower lip trembled and nudged Gram. She squeezed my bodywere's hand. The change in her was miraculous. Charlotte shook herself, wolf flaring in her eyes under the shade of her black hood before she snarled and bobbed a nod of thanks.

"Now, keep up." Gram spun, setting a wicked pace. I used to run regularly, loved to play soccer. Had fallen out of the habit. I never expected to wish I'd kept it up so I could keep stride with my frail, old grandmother.

Frail. Yeah.

Snort.

Now that Gram's magic had freed me from the gloom, I actually started to pay attention. And feel my confidence rise. We'd been walking for at least fifteen minutes and, despite passing several Enforcers in their own robes, hadn't had one moment of trouble. Not even a sniff.

Maybe this would work out after all.

I increased my pace, driving myself to keep up with Gram. In and out, chat with Ameline. Easy peasy lemon squeez—

I rounded the corner and almost meeped in shocked. Almost. Only my surprise itself kept me quiet. My head dropped immediately, though I knew I was too late.

Quaid must have seen me.

Damn it, why did he have to be here? Striding down the corridor with three other Enforcers, trainees like him with their blue piping around their hoods and sleeves? I turned my head to the side, heart racing, knowing I was totally and utterly screwed.

Came level with him, caught his scent as he brushed against me, the tingle of his power, so familiar, so welcoming.

Passed him.

Kept walking.

No. Way. Did we really just get away with it?

I glanced back quickly just as we rounded another corner to see he'd stopped. Had turned to watch us go with a frown tightening his brows.

And then we were out of sight as the stone corner cut him off.

I held my breath while Gram cursed softly, but kept moving.

No shout.

No pounding feet in pursuit.

"Damned lucky," Gram grunted.

She wasn't kidding.

"That boy is no fool," Gram said. "We have to

hurry."

Hurry I could do. All of a sudden, I felt like my feet had wings, like I could fly, adrenaline flooding my system. But Gram kept to the same deliberate, if rapid, pace and I was now forced to stay behind her, almost stepping on the backs of her fuzzy socks, an insane giggle rising inside me as I realized if anyone saw her feet they would know.

And the jig would be up.

Gram rounded one last corner and jerked open a large wooden door at the end. I looked up the narrow spiral staircase built from thick iron on the other side, feeling Enforcer magic sweep over me as I passed through the door. It paused a moment before moving on.

Still good.

"Back entry to the prison tower," Gram said. "Hope you like stairs."

I sighed and started to climb.

My thighs began to ache after twenty steps and I marveled at how agile Gram seemed to be. I reached for my magic, to make my job easier, only to have Gram's slam down over me.

"They'll know you're here the moment you tap in," she said.

Gook to know. Instead, I was forced to use my own steam. I kept my eyes locked on her socks, falling into a rhythm behind her, panting through my mouth as we made that endless climb.

I was so focused on staying in beat with her steps, I ran right into her back when she stopped. Gram spun on me with a hiss, her cheeks pink from exertion before one of her hands clamped over my arm.

"Pay attention," she said.

Her favorite chastisement. And she was right.

"This place has its own protections." Gram gestured at a second wooden door, where the stairs ended. Another window, this one gaping and wide open to the elements, allowed in a whistling breeze, the scent of desolation so powerful I almost sneezed. "It was built specifically for the Enforcers to train and to hold our most dangerous criminals. It has no desire to prevent us from entering. You understand?"

Did I ever. "Getting out might be another matter."

Gram's grim expression didn't make me feel any better.

"Stay with me," she said. "My power will protect you. But if either of you wander off, the fragments I gave you won't last long."

She might have told us that earlier. Charlotte didn't comment, face blank. I wished I was fearless like she was. But I nodded and squared myself.

Gram opened the door, the two of us right on her heels. The corridor beyond wasn't anything special to look at, more of the same, to be honest. But the feel of the place was completely different. Clingy. Challenging.

As though it weighed us and judged who we were and why we were there. I felt the power Gram gave me stir and push against the old magic embedded in the prison tower, an almost arrogant flare driving the questing magic away. I held my own energy quiet, letting Gram do what she needed to, knowing one false move would mean staying here much longer than I intended.

She moved on, the circular top of the tower bending to our right as Gram continued with purpose. She stopped so suddenly I almost ran into her again, Charlotte's hand catching me and pulling me back.

"Two guards." Gram breathed the words. Why was she risking talking? I tried to reach for her with my mind only to have her snap her finger against my wrist and shake her head.

Mental contact equaled power usage. Right.

Gotcha.

"Now what?" No way they would just let us wander in and talk to Ameline.

Gram made a face, an unhappy grimace. "I was expecting this," she said. "Just give me a second."

The wave of distaste I felt through her power told me she was about to do something neither of us would be happy about. But before I could ask her what she planned, her magic, mine tied to her, reached out to the two Enforcers around the bend.

I felt them, saw them as she did, as her power eased

around the stone wall and slid forward, tucked against the floor. It slid under their feet, winding with such subtlety if I hadn't been with her I would never have known she acted. Both Enforcers stopped moving, bodies going rigid as Gram's power took them over and held them in a soft, warm thrall.

Nothing overt. Not enough to trigger the protections of the tower. Just enough to blind them to our presence.

I could see through their eyes as Gram eased forward, knew she was in their range of sight. But all they saw was blank corridor. She turned to me, the vision snapping as she jerked me toward the door.

"You don't have long," she said. "I can't hold them forever."

Charlotte chuffed, tried to follow me to the dark metal door the two guards flanked, but Gram held her back.

"Hurry, girl," Gram said. "And you," she pulled Charlotte tight against her side, "use that nose of yours to make sure no one's coming."

Charlotte looked unhappy, but I shook my head at her before turning and touching the cold metal handle. The door sighed, magic parting under the touch of Gram's power in my fingers, the seal easing open. I drew a sharp breath, sliding inside, pushing the door closed behind me, my body registering the chill of the metal even through the thickness of the Enforcer robe and my jeans and T-shirt.

Ameline sat on a low chair next to a small table, a smile on her stunning face.

"Took you long enough," she said.

Chapter Fifteen

It required all of my forced poise to keep from wiping the smirk from her face in the most violent way possible. My demon grumbled with increasing volume as I felt one of my molars crack under the pressure of my grinding.

"The Dumont family magic was stolen," I said, skipping any kind of polite intro. Her perfect black bangs were still perfect over her smooth white skin, but one eye widened enough I knew her eyebrow arched in interest.

So Mom hadn't told her. Interesting.

Still, Ameline didn't seem surprised. Just curious. Which told me volumes.

"You had a hand in it." Accusations-R-Us.

Ameline's cold smile and small head shake, her long, black hair rippling around her, stirred my hate for her again. Even in prison she was so disgustingly flawless I could scream.

"Not I," she said. "But I do know who planned it. And knew it was coming."

No big shocker there.

"Why do you think I tried so hard to reach you?" Ameline's tone didn't match her words, coldness having nothing to do with empathy.

"To gloat." I'd finally defeated her, brought her to justice, stood here a free witch/demon/Sidhe/vampire/yada yada while she was a prisoner. So why did I suddenly feel like she found a way to win?

"As you are now painfully aware," Ameline said, stressing the word "pain" absolutely on purpose, "the information I had for you comes far too late."

Pain was Mia's Goth name. Ameline's bitch meter just jumped sixteen gazillion points.

"I, naturally, planned to act, to stop the Brotherhood." Her pink bow lips pursed, head tilting to one side, light shining from her hair as she leaned back in her chair, crossing one long, slim leg over the other. "The last thing we need," like "we" needed anything, "is for the Brotherhood to have control of so much witch magic." And she was on our side. Sure she was. "A pity you wouldn't listen when there was still time to act."

My fault.

Hell no.

"You could have told Mom." Weak, Hayle. Way to

show your soft underbelly.

Ameline didn't respond.

"They wouldn't let me come." Way worse. Way. I caught the flicker of amusement in her icy eyes, amusement burning a hole through my pride.

"You're here now," she said.

Splutter, grumble, snarl.

"I'm done with games." Gram was pretty specific about me not using magic. So I couldn't do anything against Ameline that required power.

Honestly? I wasn't beneath smacking her.

Ameline shrugged, crossing her arms over her chest, looking up at me as I approached. Attempted to loom over her. Yeah, looming takes considerable stature and I couldn't carry it off.

Didn't stop me from trying.

"I'm happy to answer all of your questions," Ameline said. "I have more information that could help in our fight against the Brotherhood."

Her little "our" and "we" stuff really started to rankle. Who did she think she was? Still, if she was willing to give up the info, I'd let her arrogance ride.

Still wanted a front seat when they burned her, though.

Oh, Syd.

"Spill it." I gave up on intimidation and copied her action, arms crossed, the heavy fabric of my stolen robe dragging on me. "I'm here, like you wanted. So tell me what you know."

Ameline's smile widened as she swept to her feet with grace I envied. "Excellent," she said. "Then let's go."

Go? "Excuse me?"

She gestured at the door. "I assume you have accomplices who can help me escape?"

She was off her freaking rocker. Being in prison must have blown a gasket or something else equally necessary to her thought process if she convinced herself, even for one bloody second, I would willingly—

"I'm not breaking you out of jail." Holy. What was she thinking?

Ameline twirled the ends of her hair in her fingertips, lashes hooding over her eyes. "If you want to know what I know," she said, "you will."

Cracked. She was totally cracked.

"I'm sorry it's been so hard on you in here," I said without a trace of honesty. "I had no idea the Enforcers shattered your damned mind so badly you think I would ever help you."

Ever.

Ameline tossed her hair over her shoulder, the plain cream robe she wore falling to her bare feet, covering all but the tips of her fingers and toes. She looked like some demented angel who'd lost her halo and wings and expected me to find them for her.

She could go to hell. Where she belonged.

"You have no idea what's coming." Ameline drew closer to me, voice low, deep. Her blue eyes held me still, not to mention the fact I refused to back down as she came right into my personal space, the scent of mint and faint flowers rising from her. "It's obvious your maji has been lax in her duties if you're still insisting on this foolishness." Ameline's hands gestured, taking in her prison. "I'm not the one to fill you in. But you will need my help, Sydlynn Hayle, before this is over."

I wanted to lean away, to step back, but I refused to show her further weakness. Instead, I tilted forward, my nose practically touching hers, nostrils flaring as I fought to contain my temper.

And my fear she really did know something I didn't.

"You'll rot in here," I said. "You and your seeds of magic." I let myself smile as her face went flat. "And when they strip you, I'll be there to do it, Ameline. I'll be there when they tie you to that big wooden stake, when they pile the kindling under you and I'll make sure they let me light the fire that burns you up."

If I hadn't been so close to her, if I hadn't been practically inside her skin, I would have missed it. But, as it was, despite how good she was at hiding how she felt, her cold veneer only ran so deep.

I saw her flinch. And it made my demon roar in triumph.

"When this all goes to hell," Ameline whispered, her breath in my mouth, "you will wish you had me with you." A tremor ran through her, anger surging, frustration. "Why do you think I've worked so hard to become maji? I could have run off and lived my life elsewhere, gathered power. The European Council would have welcomed me. I could have had my own coven by now." Fire flashed in her eyes, a hint of petulance in her voice cutting through my couldn't-care-less. She seemed momentarily confused, as if she didn't know herself why she was here, in this place, with me. But her face froze again and her resolve returned, coated liberally with ice. "Naive and pathetic." Two points of moisture hit my cheeks from Ameline's lips as she spit out those words. "There is more than one side to this story, unfolding without your knowledge. And more than one faction to deal with." That sounded so much like what Gram said about the sorcerer sects I actually started to pay attention. "You think you're the only one who has a stake in this? The only one fighting the Brotherhood?" Contempt washed over me and for the second time I had to fight to keep my position, to not retreat from her. Ameline turned her head, gaze still locked on mine, chin down as she glared from the corner of her eyes. "You'll see," she hissed. "You know nothing. But you'll need me. When you finally accept this is only the first phase of the Brotherhood's plan to control all magic on all planes, when you finally understand balance comes with light and shadow," a tingle of panic raced through me when she spoke those words, "and that only balance can win the coming war."

Light. Shadow. Trill and her brother, Owen. The young maji and her sorcerer brother were part of a prophecy, a prophecy that called them by those same names.

Ameline finally turned away, arms wrapped around herself, accentuating how slim she was as she tucked the thin fabric of her robe to her. "Ask your darling mother," she said. "Ask her if any small covens have gone missing in the last few months."

A knot, fierce and bubbling, clenched inside my stomach. "What are you talking about?"

"Tests," Ameline said, tone as light as air as she spun back, smirking again. "You idiot, they had to test their technique, didn't they?" Amusement fled, anger racing over her flawless features before she stilled again, a statue of white marble with only her flowing hair and icy eyes living things. "They've figured out a way to strip families of their magic. But they aren't stupid, Syd. Not like you. Or the High Council."

Bile burned the back of my throat, nausea churning around the lump of oh crap building inside me.

"Magical races will fall," Ameline said, old arrogance surfacing. "All of them. Without us." Her blue eyes flashed with a rainbow of power and I felt my own maji magic answer her, magic I barely kept contained under Gram's touch. "We can save them, don't you understand?" She shook her head, eyes narrowed, black lashes veils over her gaze. "But unless you free me, unless you allow me to develop as I need to develop, you will lose. And all the planes will fall to the Brotherhood."

I backed away from her, trembling suddenly, the hem of my robe vibrating as I stood there a moment and shook. She was wrong, totally wrong. Mom would never cover up something like this. And I didn't need Ameline. I was becoming maji. I could handle it.

Keep saying it, Syd. Maybe you'll even come to believe it.

I turned without speaking another word to her, knowing, unless Mom allowed me to use power against her, I wouldn't get anything useful.

Unless I broke Ameline out of prison, that was.

Her false cheer chased me out as I slid through her cell door and slammed it behind me.

"See you soon," she said.

chapter sixteen

Gram's grim expression told me my own couldn't have looked good. Instead of grilling me for answers, she hustled me around the corner and toward the exit, Charlotte sniffing at me, chuffing softly, angrily as though she could smell Ameline all over me.

Which I knew for a fact she couldn't. Hadn't been able to for ages.

Pissed Charlotte off to no end, too. I knew how she felt.

We practically ran down the stairs, Gram setting a grueling pace. My vibrating thighs and aching butt were happy to alert me to the fact I was going to suffer for a few days. Sitting down would likely be impossible without serious groaning and complaining.

But I ignored the feeling, ignored everything, let Gram lead and Charlotte follow, trusted them to keep me going in the right direction while my mind churned and the core of fear and anger in my guts writhed like a living thing.

We slowed as we entered the stronghold again, down from the tower. It was easy enough to keep my head bowed while I fought a massive battle with what Ameline told me.

I'm sorry to bear bad news, my vampire sent in a tone telling me she expected me to explode. Since nothing terrible happened, I could only assume talking to myselves in my head wouldn't trigger anything. *But there is a very good possibility Ameline is correct.*

Shut. Up.

My demon grumbled and fumed while Shaylee sighed and piped up.

Quite likely, she sent. *Though, without proof, with only her word to go on, how can we be certain?*

We are not setting her free. My demon's rumbling fury sent shudders through me. *Unless it's to find a nice place to dismember and bury her where no one will find the body.*

Iepa would have told me. I grasped onto that thought as I sent it to the others. *She would have warned me, when Trill was here. Surely she would have.* The maji who'd alerted me to the Brotherhood's impending threat hadn't said a word about Ameline. Had barely told me anything about what I was becoming. It was Trill who finally filled me in to the fact while she had maji blood, was a descendant, I was actually becoming maji.

And so, it seemed, was my nemesis.

We have to expect this transformation isn't commonplace, my vampire sent. *Or there would be new maji all the time.*

Which means we're special. My demon bared her mental teeth. *Knew that already.*

You're not helping. Shaylee's earth magic shuddered. *Is it possible?*

Light and Shadow. Two sides.

Oh. My. Swear—

Hang on, I sent as I turned a corner, Gram right in front of me. *If Ameline is meant to be maji, why is it so hard for her? Why is it such a fight?*

Silence in my head. Would wonders never cease?

You raise an excellent point, Sydlynn. My vampire sighed. *There is only one way to find out the truth. You must speak to Iepa.*

Like she would just come and chat with me over popcorn and a movie.

The maji cavern, Shaylee sent.

My demon grumbled, but agreed.

Right. The cavern under the vampire mansion, Sebastain DeWinter's home base. If I could reach Iepa anywhere, it would be there.

And then I'd have my answer.

Thanks, gang. I hugged them all, feeling the family magic coil around us, stirring ever so gently. *We'll figure this out.*

One step at a time. My vampire retreated, Shaylee's embrace full of strength, my demon's full of passion. There had been a time I feared being alone. Fearing by becoming maji, immortal and pretty much invincible was a long and lonely life sentence. But I was never alone, not really.

And despite the few occasions I wished I could have some privacy from the souls hitchhiking in my head, I wouldn't give them up for anything.

Gram faltered in front of me as we passed an opening and I only had one second to register her sudden turn toward the black before a hand reached out of the black and grabbed me, jerking me into a small, dark room. Charlotte's low growl and sudden rush of action, her wolf eyes glowing in the gloom, freed me from my captor's grip before I had a chance to react. She hunched over, just visible in the low light coming from the hall, her wolf rising as the risk to my life increased.

Craptastic.

A flare of blue light burst into life next to the shadowed shape who attacked me. Quaid's Enforcer magic, shining on his scowling face, cast unhappy shadows over his handsome features.

Yeah. The shadows were unhappy. Sure, that was it.

"What—" He stopped, cleared his throat. Ground his jaw around a moment. Tried again. "What are you doing here?"

Gram shoved past me, smacking his arm with one wrinkled hand, her magic squashing his ball of light until only a tiny fragment remained.

"You young fool!" I'd never heard her so angry, words hissing out in a powerful whisper. "What is wrong with you?"

Quaid flinched from her, but his harsh expression didn't soften. "You're here illegally." At least his voice lowered, no longer carrying out of the room and into the corridor.

"Of course we are, you absolute nitwit." She smacked him again. "Now get the hell out of the way before I squish your little soul and have it for breakfast."

Quaid quivered, shook his head. "There are rules, Ethpeal." His eyes met mine. I thought he was unhappy before. "You could have come to me."

Gram didn't get a chance to answer. Neither did I. Or Charlotte. He was lucky we were interrupted before Gram just decided to kill him and worry about the consequences later.

So lucky.

"Trainee." A woman's voice drifted from the dark, her tall, slim form emerging into the low light. She wore her hood back away from her lean face, as lined as Gram's, grim expression tossing me from the frying pan into the very hot fire.

We were cooked for sure.

Quaid bowed quickly to her. "Master Rhodes." He took a step sideways, blocking me from her full view. He needed a serious talking to if this was his idea of keeping me safe.

She waved him away, eyes locking first on me, then Charlotte and, finally, Gram.

"Ethpeal Hayle." She crossed her arms over her chest, glaring at Gram who glared right back.

"Varity Rhodes." Gram sniffed, looked the woman up and down. "You got old."

Seriously? Insults? At a time like this? If they didn't burn us at the stake for this, I'd kill Gram myself.

Varity just shrugged. "Time's been just as cruel to you, old hack."

Gram grinned, socked feet pattering on the floor as she did a little dance before spreading her hands wide for her big finale. "Still have talent, though."

Confusion twisted around shock inside me as Varity threw her head back and laughed. Just a short bark before she stepped forward and embraced Gram.

And my grandmother, my crazy, kooky, evil hearted grandmother who was in on the joke, hugged her back.

Quaid stared, open-mouthed, as Varity gripped Gram's arms in her hands and shook her just a little.

"Damn you, Ethie," she said. "You could have come to me."

Same words from Quaid.

Guess we Hayles were too independent than was good for us.

Gram shrugged and punched her friend in the shoulder. "None of your damned business," she said.

Varity turned to me, met my eyes as Charlotte eased to standing again, her wolf retreating. "Coven Leader," she said. "I've heard you had a cast-iron set, but I had no idea how big. Then again," she grinned at Gram, "you have Ethie here as a grandmother so I shouldn't really be surprised."

Quaid made a choking sound. "Master Rhodes," he said.

"Oh, hush, boy," Varity snapped. "When are they going to teach you children there is no such thing as black and white?"

I stared back and forth between the two old women, Varity's long, white hair wound into a tight braid at the back of her neck and I made a connection. "You were Gram's informant," I said. "During Mom's trial."

Varity winked. "How could I say no to that face?"

Gram beamed before jabbing Varity in the ribs. "We have to get out of here."

"Oh, really?" Her dry tone raked through the air as Varity sobered. "You think that's important, do you?"

Gram stuck her tongue out at her friend.

Varity jabbed one index finger at Quaid. "This never

happened," she said, a flare of power snapping over his shielding. "Don't make me erase your memories, Trainee Tinder."

Quaid nodded quickly. "No, Master Rhodes," he said while I wondered when he'd taken his birth parent's last name. I'd thought of him as Quaid Moromond for so long, then Quaid Dumont, hearing him use his real surname felt surreal.

Turned out we were almost to the exit anyway. I handed off my black robe to Varity who tossed the three of them into the air where they vanished. She hugged Gram quickly as Quaid hovered behind her, glancing nervously over his shoulder as Gram said goodbye.

"I'm aware of the present circumstances," Varity told me cryptically. How much did she know? "And I tell you this right now—if you need anything, Varity Rhodes is your Enforcer."

Quaid's scowl wasn't lost on me as I impulsively hugged the old woman.

"Thank you," I said. "I hope we meet under better circumstances next time."

The gateway opened, Charlotte easing through with her hand on my arm.

"I'll take that as an invitation," Varity said.

I would have felt pretty good about our escape if it hadn't been for the hurt look in Quaid's eyes as he watched us go.

chapter seventeen

I stood on the grass beside the bench and tried to pull my crap together after telling Gram and Charlotte everything Ameline told me.

Again, Gram didn't look surprised. Having her Enforcer magic with me gave her the in she needed to eavesdrop. Still, talking it out helped me work around some of my fear.

"We have to tell Mom." Why was that always my initial go-to? Old habits. But damn it, I had to talk to her. Yes, she'd freaked on me last time. And I remained rigidly furious with her. Still, now that I knew what I knew... how could I keep this from her?

And I had to know if Ameline was right. About other covens going missing.

"You're as big an idiot as that boy of yours." I didn't correct Gram. Quaid wasn't mine anymore.

Hang on. She was talking about Liam—

Oh, Syd.

"Your mother has made it very clear you're to stay out of this," Gram said. "Really feel like round two? With the information you now have, unconfirmed information that has nothing to do with the present circumstance? From a prisoner you weren't supposed to visit?"

I stared at her, muted by indecision.

"And you're going to explain where you particular knowledge came from how?" Gram smacked my arm. "Brains, girl. You were born with some. Use them."

She was right. Hell in a hand basket. I had possibly sensitive information and no way to share it with Mom. Who, frankly, was so twisted up and all kinds of wrong I was crazy even considering going to see her. Knee-jerk reaction, clearly.

Still. I had to get through to her somehow. Didn't I?

She didn't deserve the information I had.

But she was leader of the Council. She had to listen.

Like that would ever happen.

And I was arguing with myself again. Maybe Gram's nuthouse routine was contagious.

Craptastic.

After ten minutes waffling, starting out toward Massachusetts Hall before turning back several times, I finally sighed and nodded and caved.

Gram's smirk wasn't as satisfied as it was

understanding.

And so, with no other recourse, we went home.

All hail the conquering heroes.

I paced restlessly around my bedroom for hours, refusing dinner, conversation. I knew Gram filled in Shenka because I could hear them talking outside my door. Charlotte had the courtesy to stay out of my way, and I was glad. I didn't need that kind of protection.

Not the physical kind.

Just protection from myself.

I considered going to the gym, whacking on the heavy bag for a while, just to vent my frustration, but I couldn't bring myself to leave the house.

I really needed to have a bag installed in the basement.

Sleep was impossible, even well after 1AM. The quiet house finally beckoned me to emerge, now dark and quiet, the silent kitchen waking with cold light as I helped myself to some leftovers. I couldn't bring myself to go back upstairs alone, instead descending into the basement, to the family pentagram. I sat in the center, cross legged, anchoring myself in the power of the coven, feeling them sleeping through the connection.

Creepy, peeping-Tom level ickiness? Not on purpose. Just my job.

Peter Simmons tossed in his bed, a nightmare easily soothed as I sent him back to slumber. Arabelle Martin sat up reading, unable to put the book down and, for a page or so, I followed along, until the heat of the romance between the two main characters made her giggle and me blush, leaving her to her secret pleasure. Mary Gripper and her newborn son, Alex, were the only other two up so late. She didn't need me, lost in her baby, her magic embracing him, a warm cocoon of power tying back to the family, to comfort and peace and safety. All bound in love so powerful I almost wept to know what it would feel like, someday, to love someone so much.

I let the soothing feeling of her caring for her child calm me, bring me as much joy as I'd ever felt and sent silent thanks, though she would never know how much peace she brought me.

In balance at last, I dove into my exercises, the same ones Quaid helped me develop, and tried not to think about him. Would he turn me in? Turn in Varity? I found it hard to believe, knew he'd been at war with himself. But he was an Enforcer, wasn't he?

And once he took his full oath, he wouldn't owe me a scrap of loyalty.

Still, I couldn't believe he would do anything to hurt me or the coven he still called his own. It was easy to convince myself if Varity hadn't appeared, we'd still be safe. That he'd have merely vented his frustration and escorted us out. Hadn't he seemed more hurt than self-righteous, wondering why I hadn't come to him in the first place? I know he would have delivered a very firm Quaid lecture full of disappointment and opinion expressed in that jerktard way of his before simply letting us go.

The pull of creation magic cleared my mind, driving thoughts of Quaid, the stronghold, my fears and worries away completely at last. The dull, empty feeling of my sorcery woke beneath me, the petals of a dark flower opening, gaping in hunger, locking in place at the base of my power. Layers of magic, Sidhe, demon, vampire, witch, wound together in an elaborate pattern. I'd been trying different methods to connect them all, wanting to find the most efficient. I'd never been very good at the whole practicing magic thing. I always did my best work in a total panic with the fate of the world on the line. But there was something incredibly soothing about running the exercises, about absorbing myself in the flow of my powers, a feeling I embraced fully and wished I could maintain all the time.

Because that was, ultimately, the point. To reach a place where I lived my abilities, instead of reacting to them. With them.

Hopefully before the crap totally hit the fan.

The intrusion came gently, with hesitation, not really an intrusion at all. Her touch, though unexpected, was welcome and I made sure she knew it. I reached for Trill and drew her to me, letting her into the swirl of mixing magicks, amazed by the happy joy my alter egos felt at welcoming her, too. The girl I'd first met, the angry girl who hid behind a shell of harshness as her only protection, was long gone. Trust blossomed between us these days. Trill joined her creation magic to mine, the soft touch of her power sparking.

Despite her calm, I could feel her worry.

And I'd been expecting this was a social call in the middle of the night?

What's wrong? I automatically reached for answers, only to have her block me.

This is my battle to win, she sent. *I've just had some... difficulties adjusting.*

To? I sank back, hovered with her, caught the image of her sitting in the back of her family's old RV, the night sky as dark as mine, a few other vehicles outside indicating she was in some kind of campground.

Not everything is as I thought originally, she sent. *There are more sides to this puzzle than I expected.* Her fingers fiddled with themselves, reached for her face and encountered nothing.

No glasses. What happened to her that she no longer needed them?

Her use of phrase made me shudder. She felt my reaction and seized on it the same way I'd seized on hers. Made me smile.

We were so much alike it cracked me up.

I told her about Ameline, the Dumont power loss. My fight with Mom. Trill didn't feel optimistic when I ground to a halt.

I fear, she sent, a terrible fear, *Ameline is correct.*

My vampire sighed as the maji girl repeated what she'd already told me.

Aw hell.

Even as there are two sides to the sorcerer's sects, Trill sent, her mind shivering, tied to her worry, *there are those of the maji blood who don't follow our path.*

She said what? *Who are they? Are you in trouble?*

Trill's power hugged me. *I'm fine*, she sent, the "for now" she didn't add hovering between us. *But I can see now the truth of it. The Light and the Shadow, Syd. Balance. And these dark maji, they would side with Ameline and her goals.* Trill sighed mentally. *Are you certain she doesn't have good intentions? She seems determined to defeat the Brotherhood.*

If you even knew how laughable that was, I sent back. *Are these dark maji of yours well intentioned?*

Trill paused. *Excellent point.* Another moment of hesitation. *Please, be careful.*

You too. I let out my own long exhale. *Should I be guarding against these dark maji? What are they after?*

They don't know about you, she sent with a touch of panic. Like such knowledge would mean disaster. *At least as far as I can tell. You should be safe enough, as long as you don't do anything to attract them.*

Which she had, obviously. *You're sure you don't need help?*

Trill's mind echoed with gratitude. *Honestly*, she sent, *I've had better days.* She continued to shield against me and there was no way I'd pry if she didn't want me to know. As much as it killed me not to. Nosy much? *But I can handle it. And if you did try to help, they would find out about you. They'd realize we're closer to the war starting than they think. Bad enough they've misinterpreted the prophesy about Owen and I.*

Didn't sound good at all. *Okay*, I sent, *but don't be stubborn about it. If you need me, you call. We'll deal with what comes after that.*

Trill didn't say anything for a long moment and I thought maybe I'd lost her or she'd gone from me on purpose. Had I pushed her too far? I knew how proud she was, how self-reliant. I was just as bad. But when she reached for me again, I caught the image of her wiping tears from her cheeks.

Thank you, she sent, even her mental voice hoarse. *You don't know what that means, Syd. Knowing we're not alone anymore.*

Being alone was a massive touchstone for me. One I understood completely.

We sat together, minds linked, until she finally settled again. *I should let you sleep.* Like sleep was coming to me any time soon. *And I have things to attend.* Something scuttled through her power and I finally felt what was troubling her, the subtle darkness in her power. My creation magic, my maji, woke and bonded together, reaching for her, to heal the damage.

Again she blocked me. *I didn't want to admit it*, she sent. *But now that we've spoken, as much as I wanted to be rid of the dark, I think I'm going to need it.*

Balance.

Right.

You won't like this, she sent. *But you will probably need to free Ameline at some point. Be prepared.*

Like hell. *We'll see*, I sent back.

I hope not. Trill embraced me again. *But the way is dark to both of us. All we can do is what we do best.*

Save the world. I had to laugh. *Even if it doesn't want saving.*

She laughed too. *I miss you*, her mind whispered.

And then, she was gone.

I sat there a long time, fists clenched, telling myself over and over again there was no way I would ever free Ameline.

No. Way.

Never quite believing it.

chapter eighteen

Emptiness echoed from the kitchen. The touch of it pulled me from the sleep I'd finally managed to wrangle, harsh and unforgiving rest filled with endless stone corridors and Ameline's laughter.

I leaped from bed, raced down the stairs, while my heart skipped beats and adrenaline raced through my system. My power gathering, maji surging inside me. Only one thing felt empty like that.

Sorcerer.

In my house.

I skidded to a halt, iridescent power rippling around me, hands fisted and ready to attack. Gram looked up from the bubbling pot of oatmeal she stirred with a wicked little smile on her face.

"You look chipper," she said.

Someone cackled. I turned, still prepared to defend

my home. My family.

Only to come face-to-face with Demetrius's cherubic grin.

"Pretty," he said, pointing at my rainbow aura.

Gram's giggle joined his. "Think there's a pot of gold in there somewhere?"

Ha freaking ha.

I let the magic fade, the creation power easing, the many parts of me separating and falling quiet, though my demon snorted her irritation at being teased. That didn't mean I wasn't ready to turn the pair of them into something unpleasant.

Nice to know my work was paying off, though. That my maji power came out in reaction to sorcerous threat.

Shenka pounded down the stairs, running right into me, Sassafras leaping with his usual silver grace onto the table while the chuffing growl behind me told me the whole house was awake. Charlotte spotted Demetrius and heaved a sigh before turning and going back upstairs, tiny sleep shorts and midriff tank top barely covering her golden skin, muttering to herself in her Eastern European language. Swearwords. Had to be.

Shenka simply smiled, as cheery as ever, and went right to Demetrius.

"It's so nice to meet you at last," she said, holding out her hand, power dancing across her skin.

His eyes flew wide, two huge tears forming before

spilling down his cheeks. When Demetrius, facial scar pulled sideways by his grimace, leaped to his feet and wrapped his arms around Shenka, I almost laughed.

Would have if I wasn't so damned choked up. Seriously, how pathetic could he get?

And when was the last time someone treated him like a person?

Present company included.

I sank into my chair, hand drifting over Sassy's soft coat. His purr wasn't audible, but I could feel it rumble under his skin and despite its silence, his power had the desired result. By the time Gram set a steaming bowl of porridge in front of me, my mood improved from homicidal mania to grumpy.

Charlotte reappeared, dressed in her normal jeans and tight button up, sliding into a chair next to me, to my surprise. Not that I was complaining. Whatever triggered her decision to have breakfast with us, it was nice to have her there. I stopped petting Sass long enough to squeeze her hand and caught the same startled look of wonder I usually did when I treated her like she was welcome.

Jeeze. I really had to work on my people skills.

Gram served Shenka and Charlotte, a bowl of milk appearing for Sass before she sat herself and dumped half the dish of brown sugar and cinnamon on her porridge before letting me have any.

Weird, this quiet family breakfast. I didn't ask

questions, not yet. Wasn't sure why. The calm, the happy smile on Demetrius's damaged face, the way he glowed when he looked at Shenka, who kindly didn't look creeped out, even Charlotte's willingness to eat a meal with me, all added to my sense of what was right with the world.

Considering I knew what was wrong perched around the next conversation, I'd take a few minutes of happy.

I finally sighed and sat back, digging my fingers into Sassy's mane and giving him a good scratch as I focused on Demetrius. The diminutive sorcerer once freaked me out solid. As the distorted and misguided leader of the Chosen of the Light, he tried to burn me at the stake, took my magic away, kidnapped me and stole my demon. Not exactly my favorite person for a long time. But when the time came to step up and help me against the Brotherhood, Demetrius kept his word. Not to mention how hard he tried to assist me when the vampire queens had me arrested.

His smile almost gleamed, bright white teeth so perfect they looked fake as his blue eyes met mine.

"I have news," he said.

The happy bubble burst, but I didn't regret it. "Hit me," I said.

His frown made me giggle. Honestly, I'd gone from hate to tolerance to a rather odd affection for the poor man. Now that I understood how badly he'd been used, treated, just how insane he was and that there was far more to his story than Gram ever let on, I felt my heart soften further toward him as he registered I'd been kidding and bounced happily in his seat, clapping his hands together before squeezing his own cheeks between them.

Fish lips wiggled at me as he spoke. "Bet I know something you don't." It was kind of hard to make out his words, what with the whole squishing thing. But I managed.

"Let's see," I said, holding up one hand to tick off what I knew. "The Brotherhood stole the Dumont family magic." That was my index finger. "They've been testing their method on small covens to perfect it." Middle. This one sucked. I'd spent my whole life in the protected center of a powerful coven. The thought of living with such vulnerability every day made my oatmeal churn. "Mom knows what's been happening and hasn't done anything about it." Yeah, churning confirmed as my ring finger dropped. "Ameline knew all about it and I ignored her." All kinds of wrong. "And now that the Brotherhood has managed to steal one large family's magic, they'll be coming after all of us." My thumb closed around my fist just before I dropped my hand. "Am I missing anything?"

He slumped in his chair, eyes dropping to the table top, hands clenched into trembling clubs on either side of his empty bowl. "Yes," he said. "Yes, so much. Burnings and ashes and crushed bones."

Everything went still inside me. All of my alter egos froze, listened with all of our senses as a chill like the grave raced through me.

"What?"

Even Gram looked shocked, Shenka covering her mouth with one hand, eyes brimming with tears. I listened to Charlotte growl as Sassafras joined her while Demetrius bobbed his head, finally meeting my eyes again.

"Little families, so little." He tilted his head to one side, almost completely sideways, reminding me of an owl. "Such tiny magic, but it was all they needed, wasn't it? To find out. To use the machine."

"What machine, Demetrius?" I kept my voice low and as calm as possible while the phantom scent of burning flesh tickled my nose.

He hugged himself, rocking in his chair. "They took it all, all of it, right down to the bitter bits. Right down to the nasty nits." Demetrius let out a thin wail before he settled again. "Killed and butchered them, watched it all, I did, I really did. Then the fuel and the fire. And finally, the hammers and the bones in tiny little fragments." He fished in his pocket, pulling out a shard of something stained gray. I flinched back as he tossed it at me, the chunk of porous material sliding across the table to stop in front of me.

Bone. Shattered around the edges, the surface filthy with soot.

Shenka sobbed once, softly before her whole body went rigid. Charlotte bent over the sliver, snuffling while Gram sank deep into her chair.

I didn't want to touch it. But I needed to.

The moment my fingers slid over the bone, my perception slid sideways—

—*a screaming child runs from a man in a suit while fire burns behind her. A woman shrieks, voice lost in the roar of flames, arms reaching for the girl. A deep voice chuckles, strong hands lifting the weeping girl, no more than three years old before tossing her to her mother.*

To the fire. Where they both light up, their family's screams fading as the crackle of the flames devours them—

I jerked free of the vision to the sound of someone throwing up. Gram stood over Shenka, holding her hair while my second puked into the kitchen sink. Charlotte's low, hurt whining bit through my horror while Demetrius rocked and rocked.

The bone fragment slid from my fingers, rattling on the table. Sassafras hissed and spun on Demetrius.

"That wasn't necessary," he snarled.

Oh, but it was. It really was.

This family was gone. Gone forever. With the shattering of their bones, even their echoes were destroyed, their magic lost to witchdom forever.

I shoved my chair back so hard I heard wood crack. "I have proof now," I said, not recognizing the sound of my own voice, deep and harsh. "And she damned well better listen."

Gram nodded as Shenka rinsed her mouth, turning, face ashen gray, brown eyes huge.

"What are they doing with the power?" Gram's words vibrated with emotion, but she managed to hold herself together. Better than any of us.

"Don't know," Demetrius said in a sweet tone, wiping at a river of tears running down his face, tracing along the edges of his scar. "But I've seen the machine. Touched it, yes I have. Felt the magicks they keep in it." His blue eyes blinked once, slowly. "You know they went after her for only one reason."

He sounded almost sane.

"Who?" But I knew who.

Demetrius stood up. "Mia. She's weak. Always has been. The perfect test, she was, you betcha." He slid back into crazy as if his moment of lucidity never happened. "Now they know, don't they? Now they can do it and no one can stop them." He cackled, a sad, tragic sound as he bent in half and choked. "No one."

We'd just see about that.

CHAPTER NINETEEN

Charlotte had a firm hold on Demetrius the entire trip to Harvard. Not that I didn't trust him to stay with us in the veil, but one just never knew.

Would be just my luck to lose his ass in the transfer.

Gram and Shenka I left with firm instructions. We already knew the only way to combat the attack of the Brotherhood was by weakening our defenses and not giving them magic to feed their sorcery. We'd learned that lesson the hard way, when Liander Belaisle and his pack of bullies attacked the vampire mansion. But my heart still fought me, my logic, too. It felt so wrong to tell the family to let their shielding go. Not only because those shields kept us safe day to day, a natural part of who we were. But because I now had no idea if such a defense would even work against the sorcerer's new tactics.

Without the chance to have a look at this machine

Demetrius mentioned, for all I knew, lowering the family's shielding signed my family's death warrants.

I tightened my link with the coven as we stepped out of the veil and into Harvard Yard. Gram's power reached back, Shenka's too, each of the witches in my family grasping hold.

The Brotherhood had a hell of a lot to answer for.

I could tell the second I arrived Mom wasn't in her office. I spun toward University Hall and found her easily. She was with the Council, in session.

Perfect.

I didn't ask permission. Didn't care how they'd react. Fear for my family and for all covens racing through my veins, I pushed my way past the front doors and into the magicked doorway leading to Council chambers. A pair of Enforcers tried to stop me.

Tried.

I don't think I hurt them too badly.

I used just enough magic to shove them aside, honest. And burst through the huge wooden portals to thunder to a furious halt before the gaping stares of the Council.

Mom's face flashed to immediate rage, her power crackling around her, but I had no time for her temper. Not while all of witchdom was at risk. My heart went out to the families we'd lost as I faced the Council in a flare of my own magic.

"How dare you interrupt a closed meeting." Huan

Wong, the member for the Santos family, sat back in her seat, hands fluttering in front of her as her anger showed in a cascade of sparks from her fingertips. She'd never liked me, partly in thanks to the Santos's loyalties to the Dumont coven.

Tough cookies. She could hate me all she wanted, as long as she listened.

"Syd." Erica Plower, my own member on Council, clamped her jaw shut, anger flashing. She'd been Mom's second before I assigned her to Council. Old loyalties, old judgments, died hard. "What are you doing here?"

"We demand to know why you've intruded." Phylis Gaines, the tiny representative of the Bradford family glowered at me as though I were a bug she wished to squash.

"This is outrageous." That from Willa Rhodes, Rhodes coven. And similar sharp remarks from Lauren Noble of Hensley. Their individual voices were lost in the now constant, angry chatter of the Council as they talked over each other, glaring at me, aiming their unhappiness my way.

I let them shift and bubble and gather their petulant complaints. Let Mom stare me down, or try to, with her burning blue eyes. Let them seethe while I allowed my disgust and disappointment to sink into my soul and show on my face.

Children. Whiners. These were our representatives,

those who had our best interest? I didn't hear them, didn't answer them. Their complaints fell away as I narrowed my field of focus on the one person in the room who didn't say a word.

"You knew." My voice cut through their angry talk, silencing them as I shot those words like weapons at my mother. Mom didn't move, didn't respond. Didn't have to. The twitch of guilt in her face told me everything I needed to know.

"I demand to know—"

Yeah. Like I cared what Huan demanded. I guided Demetrius forward, heard them all gasp, watched him slink ahead, hunched to the side, a lopsided smile under his tears as he clung to me, a frightened but eager child whipped one too many times.

"Show them," I said. "Like you showed me." My hand went into my pocket as I reached for the magic in the room, felt the Council's power reject me at first, Mom's touch trying to keep me from what came next.

Felt her fail.

Withdrew the bone.

Lived the deaths of the coven it belonged to again. And again. And again. I didn't stop, not this time, forced them to see what I'd seen, past where Demetrius took me in my kitchen, kept my own eyes, heart, soul open even as the goodness in me withered and dried up until there was nothing left but hate.

He finally released them when I drew my arm back and threw the fragment of bone across the room. It bounced against the bottom of the Council podium, spinning like a top. I registered the sounds of the Council's sobs, their cries of horror, their magic flashing and ebbing as they struggled for control in a moment of terror, struggling with what to do next, to think.

I didn't have that problem. I had never had such clarity in my life.

And I never took my eyes from Mom's.

Instead of shock—I'd really hoped I'd see shock, wished for it like a silly child wishes with all her heart for something she knows will never happen—there was only cold rage.

Not at the Brotherhood for what they'd done. Not for the deaths of so many, for no reason, deaths that could have been prevented, covens lost that could have been saved.

No, her anger was aimed locally.

At me.

Me.

"This can't be true." Erica rose half to her feet, gripping the edge of the table for support, grief pouring out of her like the tears that ran endlessly down her pale face. "Miriam, it can't be. We would know, wouldn't we?"

Mom sat back, hands folded on the table in front of her. "I did know," she said.

Silence. Utter, deathly, overwhelming silence that tore a gaping hole in my chest. I'd assumed the entire Council was complicit. Only to discover I was wrong.

Mom had lied to all of us.

Their wailing began, rose in tempo and volume.

Because now they knew what I'd show them was true.

They ran from the room, the gathered Councilors, only Erica remaining behind. I knew where they were going, didn't have to ask. Had the same instinctual response to the news I'd uncovered. Even though they didn't officially belong to their covens anymore, gave up their family magicks to serve on the Council, I had absolutely no doubt each and every one of them ran to contact their relatives.

To make sure they were okay.

But not everyone was, were they? No, not by a long shot. How easy it was to forget there were many more families, without the power and influence necessary to demand a seat on Council. Families now diminished.

How many were gone? And did they care, these representatives of the witch world?

Doubtful. They were as selfish as I was. Focused on the ones they loved, fled to warn them, to fill them with the fear they now felt.

And Mom just sat there and glared at me like it was my fault the Brotherhood succeeded.

Erica came to my side, shaking hands taking mine. "I

had no idea," she whispered. "I swear it."

I nodded, still focused on my mother. "I know," I said. "This has nothing to do with you."

"Or you." Mom's earlier attack in her office felt like nothing as she lashed out at me vocally, a walk in the park. This Mom's rage grew like a monster around her as she stood, a vortex of magic forming at her feet as the Council power answered her need to crush me. I had no doubt, from the fury in her face, she would hurt me if she could. "And now you've ruined everything."

For the briefest of moments, I died inside as I reached for Mom and felt the same emptiness I'd encountered earlier. My mother... was my mother one of them?

Had she been taken by the Brotherhood?

But no, no, I could feel her now. She'd shielded against me, locked me out, shoved me aside like a bully on a playground unhappy her target stood up to her. I could only guess she no longer felt the need to pretend she cared anymore. Mom stalked toward me, body shaking violently as she visibly struggled to control her temper.

"Do you have any idea," she snarled, Charlotte immediately snarling back in answer, "what kind of a mess you've just unleashed?"

Even Erica gaped at her. "Miriam," she said, face paling further, her tan a dull wash over her whitened cheeks.

Mom cut her off with a sharp chop of one hand. "I had everything under control," Mom grated out through teeth clenched so tight it was hard to make her out. "And you've created mass panic. For no reason."

No reason.

No—

"If you really believe that," I whispered, her words punching me in the gut, "if you really think you have to keep the covens from protecting themselves out of your misguided fear, you've lost your damned mind." I drew myself up to my full height, not caring that my hands shook, or my voice for that matter.

"You fool," she snarled. "I can't protect them if they know the truth."

Erica gasped, backed away, shaking her head. "What are you saying?"

Mom's rage emerged in a sharp bark of laughter. "Really, Erica," she said, snapping blue eyes fixed on her oldest friend. "How naive. This Council would crumble if you knew a fraction of what threatens us."

Erica's shoulders sagged. "How do you know," she whispered, "if you don't give us the chance to find out?"

I crossed my arms over my chest as Mom looked away from Erica and met my eyes.

"I have no idea who you are," I said. "But you're not my mother."

Chapter Twenty

Erica stepped away, a sob lifting her shoulders. Mom glanced at her, breaking the hold we'd both held on each other. When Mom's eyes met mine again, she calmed enough the Council magic fell away, though I could still feel it bubbling around her edges.

"Damn you, Syd," Mom said, spinning away from me, feet thudding on the floor as she paced toward the table. "You had to disobey me, didn't you?"

"I don't believe you," I said as my own anger faded, now numb, my body dull and heavy as shock set in. Almost as if she'd physically injured me. "You let those covens be destroyed. You let Mia's magic be stolen. All to keep this quiet."

Mom's rage returned, though she had a firm hold on her power this time. She spun back, voice an unrecognizable shriek.

"I already told you, I was protecting them!" Her voice echoed in the large chamber, bouncing from wall to ceiling to floor, pummeling me with sound. "Now they are out there, stirring up their families, alerting the Brotherhood we know what they are doing. Just begging for another attack." Her hands shook as she held them out to me. "When they were clueless, they at least had their defenses up. But now? They will scatter, go to ground. Retreat further, like they always do. Cut themselves off while I've been trying to bind them together, to keep them safe through numbers." She pulled on two fists full of her long hair, manic rage in her eyes. "How am I supposed to protect them now?"

Um. Wow. Deluded much? How could she possibly think she was protecting anyone when all those witches were lost on her watch because she refused to act? Worse, where was the delusion coming from? No amount of reaching for her gave me the information I needed and I was now seriously concerned Mom had lost her crackers.

"We should have hit them first," I said, snapped, actually. "Instead of waiting for them to chip away at us a bit at a time."

Mom seemed to waver before she shook her head.

"They barely agree to work together on simple things." Mom sagged, hands dropping to her sides, desperation radiating from her. I knew how hard Mom worked to destroy old territorial lines when it came to cooperation between covens, but this was insane. "I had to keep it from them," she whispered, more to herself than me. "I had no choice. They couldn't handle what was happening." She looked up at me. "I thought I could work around the sorcerers, uncover what they were up to." Mom tried to take on the Brotherhood? Okay, I'd give her points for that. "But then the Dumont magic was taken and I had no choice."

A cover up.

She sobbed once, clutching at herself, face twisting in grief and anger. "I had it under control."

My sympathy vanished with her last words. "Your way is clearly working so very well, Mother," I said. "I say let there be panic."

Mom growled, an animal ready to attack. Charlotte tried to step in front of me, but I held her back with one hand while Mom jabbed a finger at my bodywere.

"Be careful who you threaten this time," Mom said.

"And you, Council Leader," Charlotte answered in a crisp, clear voice. "And you."

"Miriam, this is..." Erica struggled to define her feelings even as a list of words ran through my head. Horrible. Unbelievable. Disastrous.

"This is not how I wanted things to unfold." Mom turned from me, toward Erica. "Tell me honestly, if the Council knew, would this have turned out any differently?" She took a step toward her friend, Erica shaking her head as her blonde hair tossed around her face, not to say no, but in clear denial of the truth Mom shoved down her throat. "Or would they have debated and wailed and formed a committee before declaring it was a fraud until the next event." Mom was almost to Erica's side, her former second's weeping started up again as she clutched her fisted hands to her mouth. "And the next. And the next. Until it was too late. Tell me, Erica. Would you have acted?"

She turned from Mom with a sob, met my eyes.

And in hers I saw reality. Mom was right.

The Council, so tied down by law, so afraid of taking action, would have ended up in this place anyway.

"You're welcome," I said to Mom. "I think I finally managed to make them respond, wouldn't you say?"

She didn't take that very well, oh no, not even a little bit. Her power crackled again, but she didn't strike out at me. Not this time. Charlotte twitched next to me as Mom's hands clenched repeatedly as she spoke.

"You've done nothing of the sort," she said, disdain slamming into me like a hammer blow. "You've only stirred the nest. Once they've accepted what's happened, they'll go right back to their old ways."

What the bloody hell was wrong with my mother? "Then act now," I said. Almost shouted. "While you have their attention." I just wanted to shake her and shake her and not ever stop. A sick feeling preceded my next words.

"Have you even told them how to defend themselves from the Brotherhood?" Surely she'd passed out that information.

Mom's face crumpled so fast I went from rage and shock to fear for her as she backpedaled, finally collapsing against the table. Anger rushed from her, the power of the Council flaring once before it dissipated. A deep, wrenching sob ripped through her, shook her to the soles of her feet, as though her body was no longer able to maintain such rage. "Syd," she cried, "I tried." Mom pressed her shaking hands to her face, crumbling in half, falling to the floor. I rushed to her side, supported her. Mom's blue eyes, bloodshot with weeping, locked on mine. "I didn't know it was this bad," she whispered. "I swear it. And I was doing my best to keep them safe. You have to believe me."

Erica gaped at Mom, mouth opening and closing before she managed to speak. "Tell me you have a plan."

Silence.

"Mom," I said, grief rising like a tide, threatening to take over and sweep me away, "you must have known after the Dumont power was taken they wouldn't stop there." She had to have understood that.

Mom shuddered. "I didn't have proof," she said. "The Enforcers found nothing, no bones, no ash. The vision Demetrius showed us is the first real evidence we have." Her hand slid out, lifted the shard of bone resting by her foot. "And this." Her hand fisted around it as she rose, rejecting my help, using the table to balance herself as she stood, turning her back on me.

I trembled as I stood there, staring at my mother's bowed shoulders, begging her silently to act, to do something.

"Let me reach out to the other covens," I said. "I can warn them, prepare them for—"

Mom spun, face eerily composed considering she'd just been a sobbing mess, wiping tears away with the cuff of her robe. Such huge mood swings made me worry for her sanity, for all of us. "You've done enough, Coven Leader," she said, voice cold and quiet. "I now have panicked families to deal with. Thanks to you."

We were back here again, were we? "Are you kidding me?"

Mom's mouth turned down, though she refused to meet my eyes. "If you had only shown me your evidence in private," she whispered. "Syd, we're done. Go home."

I laughed. I couldn't help it. There was nothing else to do, except maybe explode. And I just didn't have the energy.

"You need my help," I said.

Mom looked up, eyes empty. "You will go home right now," she said, "or I will have you arrested."

Charlotte's snarl, her hands on my arm as she tried to tug me away told me the feeling I had from Mom wasn't imaginary. I wasn't making it up.

She was dead serious.

"This is High Council business," Mom said.

Erica's choked cry snapped us both out of our focus again. "It's High Council business," she said, "now that we know there's business needing our attention." Her eyes settled on me, shoulders squaring. "And because of Syd, we do." The angry look Erica fixed on Mom was the first time I'd ever seen her stand up to my mother. "No thanks to you, Miriam."

We all stood frozen, a tableau of blame and rage and grief. Until the doors banged open again and the Council rushed in, other witches piling in after them, screaming for answers, crowding Mom, shoving her back while she wrapped herself in the Council power and forced them all to silence.

I didn't wait for Mom to kick me out. Shoved off Maurice and his pinched dislike, pushed past the two limping Enforcers, unwilling to stand there any longer and listen to Mom lie to the people she led.

Hating I knew she was right about them.

I just hoped she took my advice and forced them to act before habit—and the fear to act—set in.

Chapter Twenty One

Home. It felt like a trap to me. Like we were sitting ducks, just waiting for the Brotherhood to show up and take our magic, burn our bodies, crush our bones.

I couldn't let it happen.

Shenka returned from visiting some of the family, only to leave again when a panicked call for support came. Not because we were under attack. But because the family was afraid.

Didn't help I was, too. And they felt it, through me. Felt my rage against Mom, my absolute loss as to what to do from here. Gram huddled in the kitchen, sock feet drawn up on her chair, hugging her knees to her thin chest, glaring into space. Charlotte constantly patrolled the house and yard, a ghost of a girl in and out of wolf form. I'd already warned Galleytrot to keep Liam safely in his cavern, away from any harm that could arise.

159

I'll watch over him, you know I will. The big dog's power hugged me, his fear as real as mine. *But what about you and the family?*

We'll manage, I sent. *I'm so close to maji, I think I can handle it.*

Liar.

Liam tried to reach me too, but I cut him off. I felt his mother in the background and just couldn't take it. Let him keep her wrapped up in Sidhe magic. Let them run through the Gate and save themselves if the time came.

I didn't have that luxury.

When I finally stopped pacing, I spun to find the only person in the house who didn't seem all that worked up making a house out of an old deck of playing cards. Demetrius stacked them with eager precision, humming happily to himself, tongue sticking out the side of his mouth, clamped between his teeth as he focused. Sassafras sat watching, tail thrashing back and forth, amber eyes on fire.

"Demetrius." He jumped at the sound of my voice, his tower collapsing in a sigh of cards. The sad look he gave me fueled my frustration. "Tell me about this machine."

Eager puppy returned. "Don't know," he said. "All crystal, all metal."

Crystal. Like the one that made Dad's statue an

unbreakable diamond and the one in my dresser drawer which saved us from the Brotherhood last time?

"So they're storing the magic." I sat at the table next to Gram, caught her head movement as she focused on me. Terrible focus. I wished she'd look away again. "But why?"

Demetrius shrugged, fingers sliding over the cards, dealing them out in an imaginary game, the soft fwap of each one landing on the table almost hypnotic. He snuffled, rubbing the side of his nose against the fresh t-shirt I'd given him to replace the ratty one he'd shown up in.

"Is there a way to retrieve magic from the crystals?" I'd been able to use mine to save Sebastian, to free him from the vampire inside me. Let it out again.

Demetrius's eyes lit up, his dealing silenced as his hands fell still. "Yes," he said. "Yes, brilliant, have I told you how brilliant and shiny?"

Gram's head whipped around. "Cough it up, nutcase."

Pot calling the kettle.

He bounced in his seat, scar pulling against his smile. "The leader," he said. "If the leader called...."

The Brotherhood made a mistake this time. Hadn't burned the bodies, crushed the bones.

They'd left the Dumonts alive.

"Mia could call it back?" I slid my chair out, ready to

run to her, to force her to listen.

Demetrius's eyes shuttered, confidence failing. "Don't know," he whispered. "Is she strong enough or isn't she?" He shook his head, white hair flopping. "Isn't she."

"Agreed," Gram said. "She's too weak to be much good for anything."

I wanted to protest. "You think if they attack a stronger coven they might fail?"

He see-sawed his hand back and forth. "Would have to kill you first," he said.

And Shenka. And Gram. And the Lawrence sisters.

And every other powerful witch in my family.

Which meant every witch in my family.

That made me feel suddenly better about our chances. One thing about our coven, we might be small, but each and every soul linked through the family magic was a force to be reckoned with. And I could only thank Gram and Mom for our strength.

Was that the biggest difference between us and the Dumonts? The fact our family was welcome to grow, expand, encouraged to be powerful as individuals while the Dumonts were crushed underfoot?

A question to be answered another time. But it reinforced the growing confidence I felt we'd fare far better than the Dumonts if the Brotherhood did come calling.

Gears rattled in my head, ground together. "Is that

why they left her alive?" Because they knew Mia wouldn't be strong enough.

And to show us what they could do.

Bastards.

"This is all a show." I lurched to my feet again, one foot lashing out to kick the lower cupboard door, sending it banging against the frame.

Demetrius bobbed his head. "They wanted you to know."

"The Dumont family needs a new leader," Gram said. Turned to me with a dark expression.

Whoa. "Hang on a second," I said. "You realize you're talking serious treason here. No coven is permitted to interfere—"

Gram slammed both fists onto the table, drawing out a hiss from Sassafras and a squeal from Demetrius. "Listen to yourself!" She stood, stalked toward me, got in my face. "You sound like your mother."

Oh no, she did *not* just say that to me.

"Syd," Sass's voice broke through my flash of rage, "Ethpeal is right." I met his amber eyes, flickering back to glare at Gram. "Mia is too weak. If there is even a chance the Dumont family magic can be restored and the other powers can be stripped from the crystal machine, she must be replaced with someone who can seize back control."

I knew they were both right. Of course they were.

163

But, damn it, this was Mia.

My friend.

And as a coven leader, the very idea made me want to puke up the soles of my feet.

"I'll take you." Demetrius slid from his chair, hands twitching at his sides. "I know where it is."

Well, that little piece of info would have been handy. "We could tell Mom." Sigh. "The Enforcers could deal with it."

Gram turned her back on me. "Then we fail," she said, sinking into her chair again.

Demetrius bobbed his head. Pointed at me. "A strong leader, the magic, yes. It should work. But you, we need you, Maji." He whispered the last to me as though in worship. Creeped me out.

"No." Gram hugged her knees again. "While your mother's methods are questionable, she's right. You have to stay out of this, especially this." Her voice quavered, sounded like an old woman's. Since when did Gram give up?

"Screw that," I snarled as Sassafras snapped his tail around his paws.

"I'm with Syd," he said. "But who can we approach?" His tongue groomed one paw three short strokes before he settled again. "Ameline is in prison."

"And staying there." Not even thinking about it.

"The most despised Odette is dead." Sass didn't

sound that upset. Gram snorted, bared her teeth at him. "All of the strong Dumont women are gone."

Gram let out a gusty sigh, feet thudding to the floor while Demetrius hopped on one foot, eyes locked on her. "There's only one person of any power and respect of the family remaining."

I couldn't think of a single woman.

"Andre." Gram grit her teeth, heels thudding against her chair legs.

A man? "Unprecedented." Sassafras's snort of derision beat me to it.

"Perhaps," Gram said, "but as long as the family magic accepts him, he's leader."

Were we really considering putting Odette's only son, our enemy, in control of the Dumont family?

"We could set up our own leader." Someone to support Mia, even for a little while.

Sassafras's amber magic snapped at me, making my demon hiss. "Don't be an idiot," he said in Gram's exact tone. "What we're discussing here is bad enough. If we are even remotely tied to the takeover of the Dumont family power, instrumental in any kind of rebellion against Mia, you'll be on fire before you can ask what's burning."

Gram tapped her nails on the table, the sound adding to my tension. "As much as I can't stand his weasel ass," she said, "at least he's pure Dumont. And as powerful as any female witch of his line." I hesitated to say "was". Gram hadn't felt him after the attack. Which made me groan inwardly. The weakness I'd felt in the Dumonts—was that due to the Brotherhood's tampering or their own inherent lack of power as I'd begun to wonder? And either way, did that mean Andre wouldn't have the strength to free the coven magic after all?

There was only one way to find out.

"I agree," Sassafras said like that wrapped up the matter. "Andre it is."

There had been so much betrayal in my own life in the past several years. Could I do this to Mia?

Ultimately, my heart told me no.

"We have to give her the chance," I said at last. "Before we do anything, Mia has the right to redeem herself."

Gram looked like she wanted to argue, but Sassafras was the one who spoke.

"We might only get one chance," he said, voice level, eyes glowing demon fire. "Are you sure you want to use it on Mia?"

"It's her coven," I said, hardening myself against the fact I expected her to fail. I'd be there for her, to support her. We'd make this work. And I knew I could convince her to come with me and not try to charge me with interference. I didn't trust Andre as far as I could chuck his Armani-suited Dumontness.

Even if I tried to help him, it was likely he'd turn on me just for spite.

Mia it was. "Weak or not, Mia is the leader of the Dumont family," I said. "For all we know, she's the only one the power will go to anyway. So it has to be her."

They grumbled and mumbled and sighed. But they agreed, trusting me.

I just wished the feeling was mutual. I could have used a little self-trust right about now.

chapter twenty two

I took a moment to slip out to the back yard, to gather my thoughts and pull myself together. The instant my butt hit the bench, I thought of Mr. Yummy Leather Pants and how this was Quaid's and my usual meeting place. Or had been. Followed by a dose of guilt and worry about him. I'd left him in a precarious position. And while he wouldn't have survived turning me in if that had been his intent after all, it really wasn't his fault I broke the law.

He'd told me in autumn, if I needed him, no matter what, he was there for me. Which made my initial worry he would tell on me anyway fade to non-existence. If Quaid was going to play rat fink, he'd have done it long before now. That look he'd given me in the corridor back at the stronghold, told me he'd known it was me all along.

And rather than sending in the cavalry to round me

up, he waited in the dark, alone, to corner me himself.

As much as I wished it wasn't true, I needed him now. It was likely what I was about to ask of him would put him in the line of fire with me. At least he had Varity to protect him if anyone found out about our little invasion. But if he answered my call this time, he was on his own.

I briefly considered contacting the Rhodes Enforcer instead. She'd offered, after all. And proven herself more than trustworthy. But the selfish part of me wanted Quaid, the familiar feel of his power, while I argued with myself I already knew how to work with him and didn't have time to wrangle a new Enforcer.

Yeah, that was the reason.

I think he was waiting for me, because the moment I reached for him he reached back, the warm deliciousness of him sliding over my magic.

Are you all right? There was a time he would have asked me what kind of trouble I was raising with a jab of judgment or gone right into a lecture about our last encounter. But he'd mellowed in the past year, worry and concern replacing his jerkishness.

Damn it. This would be easier if he wasn't all nice and stuff.

I'm fine, I sent. *But I have news.*

If you're referring to the Brotherhood, he sent with a hint of his old sarcasm, *I don't think there's a witch on the continent*

169

that isn't aware of the threat now. Nice going.

Ah, there he was. My faithful jerkasaurus.

You sound like Mom, I snapped. *Would you rather stick your head up your ass and wait for the Brotherhood to destroy everything?*

Not in the least. His sarcasm faded. *I meant it. Miriam might think she knows what's best for us, but the time comes when a little freaking out gets the job done faster than trying to be subtle.*

Oh. Okay then. Weird. He never agreed with me.

I shared what Demetrius told me, about the confrontation with Mom. He winced mentally, but didn't comment until I was done.

You realize even approaching Mia at this point could be seen as interference. I felt his physical body moving, coming closer. He fell silent a moment, blocking me, the muffled feeling of another mind in his rumbling through. I waited, gnawing on my quick-chewed nails, feet swinging under the bench in the soft sunshine until the wah-wah conversation ended and he came back to me.

It's not my first time on the disobedience rodeo circuit, I sent as soon as I had his attention. *But if Demetrius is right, this could be our chance to stop the Brotherhood before they attack another family.*

Which could happen at any second. Frankly, I had no idea what they were waiting for.

Gave me a serious jolt of anxiety to think about it.

We don't have much time. He was moving again, mental

voice intense. *I was just told Enforcers are being dispatched to watch over the families. Two teams of two.*

Took her freaking long enough to act. And when she finally did? Yeah, perfect timing, Mom.

Get here as fast as you can, I sent, standing and turning to the door. *We need to move before they arrive.*

A rush of air displacement at my back spun me around with one hand on the door. Quaid strode out of the flash of blue light, already shedding his black robe, tight jeans and crumpled t-shirt revealed underneath.

"My thought exactly," he said as he tossed his robe over one arm before stepping into my space.

We didn't have time for—

Made time. For lips like that?

Liam crossed my mind. His control freak mother.

My choice. Quaid's.

All of it, gone under the pressure of demanding lips, the crush of his magic as he pulled me tightly to him, the pulse of his heart under my hands through his thin t-shirt. The heat of his skin, the way his soft hair sifted through my fingers. And his breath.

Inside me.

My demon uncoiled, drew him closer, one leg lifting to hook around his hip. Quaid leaned in, pressing me against the door, big, hot hands under the hem of my shirt, sliding over my back, under the strap of my bra.

Quaid.

Oh dear.

He leaned away, the tip of his nose tracing over my cheekbone before his dark chocolate eyes opened and met mine. Fire burned inside them, fire my demon matched, begged to ignite into a roaring inferno. To forget in him, to be part of something bigger and sweeter and so delicious I knew I could survive anything as long as I had Quaid.

Tears prickled, my throat tightening as I pulled away. That was the problem, wasn't it? I didn't have Quaid.

Never would.

The fire died slowly, painfully, my demon turning her back on me in disgust and frustration while Quaid bowed his head, black, wavy hair tossing as he looked away.

"I take it you need me to contact Mia for you." His voice sounded husky, rough and heavy. I wanted so badly to touch him, to stroke his skin, take his hand, lead him upstairs to my room. But the bubble had broken, the lure's need retreating and the magic we shared between us fading into nothing again.

I thought he was my destiny once. Was told that was the case.

Try as I might, I couldn't seem to shake the feeling no matter how many times I committed to ending it, we'd never be over.

And that broke my heart.

I cleared my throat, stuffing my hands into the back

pockets of my jeans to keep from touching him again. "Smart cookie is smart," I said, lips twitching into a smile. "When did that happen?"

Quaid's wide lips lifted, dark eyes still full of sultry promise though the smirk added a more familiar edge to his appeal. "Hilarious, Hayle," he said. "Wow, I had no idea you were so funny. You must have been working on it lately."

It was hard not to giggle. I punched his arm, sighed out the last of my emotional overflow and bobbed my head.

"We'd better get moving," I said.

Chapter Twenty Three

Gram didn't seem at all surprised Quaid was with me when I reentered the kitchen. She fixed him with her faded blue eyes, not moving as he bent over her and soundly kissed her cheek.

"I wouldn't have turned you in, crazy lady," he said, deep voice rumbling in the quiet.

"Hrumph," she said, swatting at him, wiping at the place his lips had been like he gave her cooties. But when her gaze met mine, there was a sparkle in it that had been missing since we started our little discussion about the Dumont succession.

"You two go," Gram said. "At least Quaid will have an excuse and he might be able to make one for you if you can get to Mia before her watchers do."

Charlotte didn't ask. Didn't have to. Like she'd let me leave her behind.

"You'll have to cover for us," Quaid said. "Miriam assigned two Enforcer teams to each coven."

Gram's face screwed up in a scowl. "Lot of good that will do now," she said.

Hadn't I just had the same thought?

I felt the arrival of our new watchdogs just before we stepped through the veil. Gram would have no problem handling them, I knew. Besides, if Mom expected to fence in entire covens with four Enforcers, if her plan was to keep us all prisoners in our own homes, she had another thing coming.

And I honestly had no doubt in my mind such was the case. The grim look Quaid gave me as we emerged from the veil on the Dumont property told me he assumed the worst too.

We need to come together, I sent to him as he extended his Enforcer power around Charlotte and I. *Not sit in our own little segregated families and wait it out.*

I agree, he sent as blue flames licked around me, the flash of light so bright I had to squint my eyes closed. *But she's Council Leader. And the covens are scared. Do you think they'll try something new or fall back on the old ways at a time like this?*

The idiots. He was right. They'd slink down into their hidey holes and hope this all went away.

I didn't have that luxury. Or want it.

Shocking.

175

While the veil deposited us behind the Dumont mansion, Quaid's power landed us right in Mia's bedroom. I heard her shriek and lunged for her before she could freak out further, Quaid joining me as Charlotte fell back to snuffle around the room, stopping with her ear to the door.

Mia fell against me the moment she realized who I was, reaching then for Quaid, sliding her arms around his neck. She sobbed on his shoulder, bruise-dark circles under her eyes, pale skin almost transparent. Her crystal blue gaze locked on me as she clung to her brother.

"Thank you for coming to visit," she whispered. Clearly forgetting she'd thrown me out the last time I was here.

Sigh.

Quaid eased her gently back, carrying her over to the window seat where he knelt beside her. White hands twisted into knots while warm, tanned ones, twice her size, folded around her fingers and pressed tight.

"Mia," he said, "we have a plan to take the Dumont family magic back. But we need your help to do it."

He might as well have told her she'd just been crowned empress of the world. Mia's downcast expression vanished, absolute joy washing over her as she lunged at him again, hugging him so tight I thought his head might pop off.

"Really?" She looked up at me, an excited six-year-old

on Christmas morning. "You know who took it? Where it is?"

I let Quaid do the talking, staying out of it as much as I could. For obvious reasons. At least this way if someone tried to call interference, I could honestly say I didn't open my mouth once. Mia was so wrapped up in Quaid's explanation she barely looked my way again until he was through.

Jaw set, a new determination lighting her face, Mia pushed herself to her feet. A thin thread of hope wound itself around my heart as she stepped away from her brother's support and met my eyes.

"I'm ready," she said, voice quivering despite her surge of strength. "Just tell me what to do."

I couldn't help the smile lifting my lips. Maybe I was wrong about Mia. If she survived this, won back the Dumont family magic, it was likely she would finally become the leader they needed. Surely this kind of trial by fire would help her find her backbone.

As much as this was a disaster and a mess, it just might turn out for the best in the end. The thought the Brotherhood's plan might have shot them in the foot made me want to hug myself and giggle like a little kid.

We were a long way from celebrating yet, though.

"We have to making it past the Enforcers guarding the house." Quaid glanced at Charlotte who shook her head at him, coast clear. "I can't carry all of us out at once."

"It's my house," Mia said, straightening her shoulders, wiping at the tear-tracks on her cheeks. "I'll leave it if I want to."

Mia found her spine? Check.

Wicked.

We didn't make it half-way down the hall before we were discovered.

"And where are you off to, *mon chef?*" I scowled at Andre who slipped out of a side door to stand in front of us. His blue eyes traveled over me, Charlotte, Quaid and finally settled on Mia. "In such illustrious company."

Mia's chin began to quiver, hands clawing at her sides. "Stay out of my way, Andre." Her newly-acquired spine seemed to have some cracked vertebra. "This is none of your concern."

He tsked softly into the quiet air. "*Au contraire*," he said. "The safety and security of my leader is most definitely my concern." Icy eyes landed on me. "Wouldn't you agree, *cher?*"

Damn him. We were doing this for his benefit too, the slimy ass. I wanted to respond, to act, but I couldn't, gagged by the need to stay out of it, if only verbally.

"I'm going to retrieve the family magic." Mia said it like she was off to the store for some milk and did he need anything else? Andre's arched eyebrow lifted, handsome, angular face so surprised all the arrogance washed out of him for once.

But when he spoke again, he wasn't looking at her. Nope. Those blue Dumont peepers were fixed solely on yours truly.

"We have never been friends," Andre said, voice low and accent thick, as though emotion affected his English, "and, indeed, have been enemies. But I tell you now, Sydlynn Hayle, if you can accomplish this thing, the Dumont family will owe you a debt we will never be able to repay."

Straight up. I bowed my head to him, just a little, as Mia's eyes snapped angrily at me.

"We need to leave," she said. "And we could use some help."

Andre didn't hesitate. "Come this way."

Why was I not surprised there was a secret exit from the back of the house? Likely many secret exits. This was a nervous family, apparently.

And as I tore open the veil, turning to see Andre watch us go, I fought with the understanding he wasn't the enemy. Just another witch tied to a system forcing us to hide and plot and work behind the scenes.

No, the real enemy was ahead of us.

And they better look the hell out.

Chapter Twenty Four

Mia shivered in my kitchen while Gram gave her the once over. I didn't have the time to coddle the Dumont leader, not while Demetrius linked his mind to me to show where we were going.

"A high rise?" The looming sky scraper towered over a city I didn't know. My fear of heights triggered as he swooped my view toward the base of the building, flinching as we almost impacted it only to fly upwards like some mental roller coaster, passing row after row of windows as his mind led mine all the way to the top.

Where we slammed into a barrier of emptiness, bouncing back from it so hard I snapped out of the vision.

Demetrius shook his head, staggering. "Oops," he said. "That's new."

A fireball headache burst behind my eyes before slowly fading into a dull ache.

"The roof?" I pressed my hands to my temples.

Demetrius bobbed a nod. "All the way to the top," he said.

Of course it was. Wouldn't do to have their weapon of mass magic destruction on the ground or anything. Put it up on the pinnacle of some giant building where falling was a real possibility.

Wasn't afraid of heights, I realized. Just the ahhhhhhhh splat at the end.

Gram's faded blue eyes narrowed. "We have to do something about that little problem of yours someday," she said.

Leave it to her to know exactly what I was thinking. Quaid frowned, but I ignored the questioning look behind his worry and shrugged in the fading light of the setting sun. We'd lost the whole day already. Time to get moving.

In the dark. My favorite.

Why couldn't bad crap happen in the morning for once? Just to break up the creep factor monotony?

Demetrius pointed at my hand. "You need it," he said.

Right. I ran upstairs to my room, and rooted around in my underwear drawer until my fingers encountered cold stone. The crystal pulsed in my palm, waking as I touched it, bubbling with happiness like an eager puppy, its tiny soul bouncing and wriggling in pleasure. More guilt. I'd been ignoring it lately, despite the fact I knew it was alive—or as alive as something inanimate could be, thanks to the power of the vampire essence. She soothed it personally, helping it settle, her cold, white magic pulsing inside the crystal until the wee soul calmed. I still felt it tickle against my hand as I slid it into my pocket, the chill of it warming to my body temperature.

I really had to take better care of it. And, as I hustled back down stairs, I had my second epiphany in this madness. I worked the exercises to connect to my maji power and had done so, but the maintenance of that power, the final connection, always evaded me. I admitted to myself there was serious shudder factor tied to my sorcery, holding me back. But the crystal would make things much easier.

Gram was right. I really was an idiot sometimes.

Demetrius clapped his hands in excitement when I returned to the kitchen and let him see my prize. One finger stroked it gently, a spark of white magic jumping between them.

"Excellent," he said in a clear, crisp voice, jumbled mind coming together in lucidity for a moment. His whole body shifted, shoulders going back, face serious. "Though I wish you'd spent more time with it, Sydlynn. Your tie to the crystal is the support system for your sorcery. Not necessary, but definitely an advantage."

Yammer yammer. I already beat myself up about this, thanks.

The kitchen door opened as I looked up, met Shenka's eyes. She looked tired, but determined and I was again thankful I chose her for my second.

She took one look at our little group, at Mia shivering, Quaid standing over his sister and nodded. "I take it you're off again."

No resentment. Just support. I loved her so much in that moment, I went to her and hugged her, feeling the warmth of her arms as she hugged me back.

I need you to stay out of it. Tears prickled in my eyes, my chest tight as I held on to her. *If this goes bad, and there's a good chance it will, I need to know you're here. That someone I trust can protect the family.*

She clung to me as much as I to her. *I want to come with you*, she sent. *But I'm your second. And I've known all along what that means. That you, my crazy friend with your crazy life, will always be running off and I'll be here, making sure home is still here for you to come back to.* Shenka leaned back, smiled bravely. *I'll die before I let anything happen to our coven, my leader.*

No way I was crying. No. Way.

Sniffle.

"Are we doing this, or what?" I turned and met Quaid's eyes, voice gruff with emotion, needing to go before I broke down into a weeping mess resembling Mia. Charlotte hovering behind the tall Enforcer trainee. To my surprise, Sassafras leaped the distance between himself and my bodywere. She caught him easily, lifting him to lie across her shoulders.

"You're not coming," I said.

"Try and stop me." He dug his claws into the leather of Charlotte's jacket. "We have no idea what you're walking into. And I refuse to let you go without backup."

Considering I had Quaid and Charlotte, not to mention Demetrius's considerable sorcerer abilities, I was hardly alone.

Until I thought about the empty place we headed to.

"This is a bad idea." My hand fisted around the crystal. "There's a very good chance none of you will have access to your magic where we're going."

"All the more reason I should join you," Sass said. "If it comes to a fight we're losing, I can run for help."

Insufferable ball of fluff. "That's stupid," I said. "If we're in a fight we're losing, we all run for help."

Gram snorted, but shook her head at me. "Take the cat," she said. "He has more resources than power at his disposal."

Fine. Whatever. I was surrounded by stubborn.

Wonder where I got it from.

The night air had cooled, a skim of moisture squeaking under my sneakers as I crossed the dew-laden grass of the backyard. Gram's magic, tied to the family and to me, bubbled over us. I could feel that same protective touch she'd used in the Enforcer stronghold slide outward, this time forming a kind of generalized lack of interest as well as a false image. I glanced up and to the right, caught sight of two Enforcers hovering on the roof. Neither looked our way, staring out over the street.

Good thing someone was paying attention. I totally forgot they were here.

"Be quick," Gram said. "I can't fool all four of them for long." She winked. "Without doing some damage, that is."

Quaid gaped at her. Gram giggled and smacked him on his very attractive ass, ending her blow with a little pinch to his tightly-jeaned right cheek.

"Didn't teach you this trick yet, did they, boy?"

Quaid's surprise vanished, a wicked grin on his face as he bent and kissed her on the corner of her mouth.

"Know it now," he said.

Gram's wicked cackle made me grin. Despite the desperate situation, despite where we were going, I could still find joy in the most amazing places.

Mia wasn't quite so able. "Can we go?" She shivered beside her brother, eyes huge, face sunken and ghostly white in the low light over the back door.

Right. Fun time over.

Without another glance at the now useless Enforcers,

knowing Gram had my back, I crossed the last few feet to the edge of the park and sliced open the veil. Quaid took my hand, Mia his, Demetrius reaching for my other while Charlotte tucked in on the end, both hands around Mia's waist while Sassafras clung like a fur stole to the weregirl's neck.

All aboard. Hands and feet inside the Syd at all times. Here we go.

I opened to the emptiness of Demetrius, felt his power touch my crystal—and he wasn't empty anymore. I saw the building, felt the path, dove into the veil.

Just as Trill's mind touched mine.

Syd—

She was gone, her mental connection severed by the rubbery membrane between planes. That one word, my name, had concern behind it, real fear. Was she in trouble? I had no way of knowing. Not while we slid through the darkness.

My demon welcomed the touch of the Node, the source of balance on Demonicon, and I paused one moment to embrace the warmth of its power as it drew me close, the tang of my demon grandmother's soul alive and well. Ahbi's power wished me well before the veil tore once again and we were free.

chapter twenty five

I stepped out into a warm night at the entrance to a busy street. The humid air hit me immediately, moisture standing out on my skin. Jeans were too heavy, my t-shirt the only saving grace. I heard Sassafras hiss, glanced over to watch his fur puff up as Charlotte gently slid him from around her neck and cradled him against her side with one arm, shedding her leather jacket from the other.

"Where are we?" I turned to Demetrius, hoping he'd maintained his sanity long enough to get us through this mess. Instead, I found him hopping up and down, from foot to foot, hands pressed to his mouth as he giggled silently into them.

"Sunshine state," he said.

Florida.

"Looks like Miami." Quaid pulled Mia against him, one arm around her shoulders as she slumped in the heat.

"We lived here once, when I was with the Moromonds, a long time ago."

I looked up, up at the building, now familiar, reached for it with my power.

Came up empty. No pun intended.

"The whole building is warded now," I said.

Demetrius stopped his crazy dance and swallowed so hard I heard him.

"That means," I said to the others, "I was right about your magic. You'll be powerless." I met Charlotte's eyes. "All but you, apparently."

She nodded. "The power in the Brotherhood house had no effect on my abilities," she said. "I don't know why."

Demetrius bobbed a nod, making "Ooh! Ooh!" sounds and raising his hand like an eager kid at the front of the class. I sighed. This was going to be a long night.

"Go ahead," I said.

"They made you." Demetrius clapped his hands quickly, a rapid-fire applause. "So you're immune."

Charlotte flinched, scowled so deeply even I was surprised, leaned toward the grinning little man with her wolf distorting her face.

"Liar," she snarled. "We were not made by sorcery. We were born from greater things."

Well, that was interesting. But Demetrius either didn't take the werewarning or didn't care, because he reached out with one finger and touched the tip of her nose. Even made the "boop" noise.

"We really need to talk," he said in his lucid voice before cackling like a crazy person.

"Later," I said, as a pair of pedestrians, replete in walking shorts and really hideous matching shirts, their elderly appearance and large camera marking them as tourists, glanced our way. The woman gasped before hurrying her husband along. I looked around at our little group, Charlotte still in mad-were mode, Demetrius bobbing like a whack-a-mole, Mia's ghostly appearance.

Freak show, coming through.

I led them into the street anyway, through the wandering tourists, to the sound of cars passing, the thrum of music coming somewhere to the right. I smelled the salt tang of the ocean, different than the Pacific, but welcome nonetheless. I knew my family would never be able to move again, not with the Wild Hunt sleeping under the back yard, but I really had to consider a summer place by the sea.

We stopped at the crosswalk to wait for the light amid a small group of pedestrians. Most took a side-step away from us, but a pair of teens in jeans to their knees and sporting headphones in their ears both flashed us a wave, the first one winking at me with a wolf-whistle.

Classy.

Charlotte's snarl sent my suitor back a step, Quaid's

looming anger sending him scurrying so fast he ran into his friend and knocked them both off balance.

We really had to get away from the normals before someone did something to get us arrested.

Demetrius took my hand as the light finally shifted and we crossed. I had a sudden understanding of what it would be like to be a mother with a bratty kid. He tugged at me, tried to wander off, poked at other people crossing in the opposite direction, giggling and dancing the whole way. I caught myself rolling my eyes as I met Quaid's and he grinned at me like it was funny.

If we made it out of this, I was making Quaid hold Demetrius's hand on the way back.

The building loomed over us, the entire city crushing down on me, the stars lost in the bright lights from the skyscrapers, the street lights. It felt like another plane, almost like I'd somehow crossed over the veil instead of sliding through it. I didn't mind cities, not really. I'd been to a few. But I'd never spent any amount of time in one on this plane, and now I realized I had no desire to. My magic wanted to go on overload, so many people to shield from. My demon snarled as a guy came close to bumping me, only to come in contact with Charlotte's shoulder.

He scowled at her until she growled back.

Yeah, I really had to get them off the street.

The glass doors beckoned, the interior of the building

brightly lit on the other side. I pushed against the heavy metal handle, feeling it give easily, the hiss of escaping air cold on my skin as the air-conditioned interior called me inside.

The moment my feet passed the threshold, my power went dead. Out like a light. I knew it was coming, expected it. And it still drove a giant shard of "hell, no" through me. No demon, no vampire. No Shaylee. No family magic.

The shocked look on Quaid's face, on Mia's, told me I wasn't the only one.

"Deep breaths," I said quietly. "It takes a second for the panic to wear off."

Quaid's chocolate eyes were almost completely black as his pupils flared in response to his anxiety. "This is. Syd. This is..."

"I know." I slid my hand into his while Demetrius, untouched by what was happening to the rest of us, pulled on my other one with little grunting noises. "You can leave. I'll be okay."

He shook his head, squeezing my fingers before letting my hand go, his jaw clenching. "I'm fine," he said. Hugged Mia. "We have a job to do."

Mia shook so violently in his grip I thought she'd break down any second. Maybe explode. Or implode. Or something violent. But, as she stood there, she calmed, clinging to her brother until she nodded once, a sharp gesture, biting her lower lip so hard she had to be drawing blood.

"I have to get my magic back."

One quick look at Sassafras shivering in Charlotte's arms and I knew he was still in.

"So wrong," he said. "Hurry up."

Right. I let Demetrius win, finally, looking up as we entered the large foyer, feeling my feet squeak over the polished floor. A bank of elevator doors stood on the right and another on the left while a bulky desk dominated the middle of the lobby. A man in uniform frowned at us as Demetrius bypassed him.

"Hey," he called out. "This isn't some tourist spot. You need an appointment."

Demetrius didn't even twitch. The man froze, sagged and sank back into his seat. I shivered as we passed, the vacant look on his face making me worry about him.

But I couldn't worry. He wasn't my problem.

We were almost to the elevators on the right when Quaid stopped me with a hand on my arm.

"Is this the best choice?" He glanced at the shining steel doors. "We could get trapped in there."

He was right. But the idea of climbing all the way to the top... I groaned, my legs and butt still tender from the prison tower.

Still.

Demetrius grunted and shrugged, crossing to the back

of the lobby and a wide, black painted entry with a stair symbol hanging over it. The door whispered open, a concrete staircase, metal railing leading upward, waiting on the other side.

Climbing, then.

I took the lead, foot taking the first step just as my hand closed reflexively over the crystal in my pocket.

And everything shifted.

They were back, my demon roaring her happiness, Shaylee babbling my name, my vampire hissing and reaching for me. The family magic swirled, wrapped around me while my sorcery opened its dark blossom at the base of everything. The tiny heart of the crystal sang to me as my maji power woke and brought us all together as one.

Whole. I grinned at Quaid before taking the steps two at a time, letting the power I'd woken feed me.

This was what it was supposed to be like.

Time to kick some Brotherhood ass.

Chapter Twenty Six

The tiny pop of electricity preceded me and it wasn't until I noticed the small surveillance camera on the fifth floor landing, black smoke pouring out of its casing, I realized Demetrius was keeping the Brotherhood from tracking us.

I'd seen enough cop movies to swear inside my head at myself for not thinking of it first.

It was a long climb, but seemed to fly by, floor after floor disappearing beneath me. I'm absolutely positive if I didn't have access to my magic I would never have made the climb. Even with the boost I was a panting, sweating mess by the time we reached the top. Charlotte looked a little ruffled, as though she'd exerted herself in a brisk run. Her breathing returned to normal as she shook herself, setting Sassafras back on the ground. Demetrius, I decided, was completely tireless, as eager as he'd been all along, now pulling on me again as I stopped to catch my wind at the top of the stairs.

Mia leaned heavily on Quaid who looked about as worn out as I was, probably because he'd been forced to carry his sister most of the way. I felt a pang of guilt. I hadn't even thought about them in my race to the top. A wash of power rectified the situation, though from Mia's wide stare and the sudden flash of anger on Quaid's face, it was too little, too late.

"Nice of you to let us know you have your power back." He eased Mia to the floor, dark eyes snapping with anger.

Wince. I offered him more power, his body straightening, Mia's bright red face easing back to deathly pale. Not really an improvement.

"The crystal." I showed it to Quaid, took his hand, pressed it to the stone on impulse. His whole body jerked, magic flaring in his eyes before shutting down again. "I think this was the last piece I needed."

Quaid's anger faded as he nodded. "Makes sense," he said. "All the exercises in the world won't allow you to be full maji if you aren't fully connected to all of your power sources." He stepped back, shaking the hand I'd pressed to the crystal. "At least one of us won't be magickless."

"You and Sassafras stay here," I said. "With Mia. When we've found the machine, we'll come back for you."

Mia shoved herself to her feet while Sassafras smacked my leg with one paw.

"I'm coming with you," Mia said as my silver Persian muttered something distinctly rude and unrepeatable.

Quaid didn't have to talk. He just glared and I got the message.

They were all as bad as I was when it came to leaping head first into trouble. And wouldn't I have fun rubbing Quaid's face in that fact when this was over?

As long as we lived to talk about it.

Demetrius's hand lifted, a small crystal of his own gripped in his fingers. He leaned into the steel door, pressing the stone to the keypad beside it. A release of air and the tang of ozone and the small silver box slagged, liquid metal pouring out from under the panel, the keys oozing in white plastic rivers. Something snicked and Demetrius grinned his maniacal happiness, scar pulling his face into creepy.

"Ready?" He jerked on the handle, long before I could tell him that no, actually, as a matter of fact, I was nowhere near ready and could we just turn around and go home and think this through again maybe? Instead, I found myself rushing forward, crystal firmly in hand, my power lashing out at the hulking, suited sorcerers guarding the other side of the door.

We took them by surprise, oddly. I thought for sure they would have felt us coming. Either that, or these two were totally out of touch with reality. Luck was on our side as Demetrius, snarling and snapping like a vicious little animal, dove for the first one while I jerked on my whip of magic and pulled the second to his knees before lashing out with my foot, my heel impacting the side of his wide jaw.

He didn't even get a chance to fight back. Eyes rolling into his head, the guard groaned softly and sagged to the left, collapsing onto his friend who Demetrius had just sent into his own oblivion.

Quaid's raised eyebrows and little smirk told me he had no idea I'd been hitting the gym.

Yeah, that's right, buddy. Look out.

I wondered if he'd still be smiling if he met Sage.

Snort.

No time to be smug. Charlotte leap-frogged the two fallen guards, jacket discarded, jeans tearing as she shifted into half-wolf form. While I'd been patting myself on the back for one kick boosted with magic, she noticed the real danger.

Two more guards lunged for us from across the narrow hallway. And Charlotte lunged back.

Claws glistening in the dim fluorescents, she slashed the first across the throat with one hand while driving the other into the chest of the second. Blood gushed, pinpoints of moisture tagging my face and neck as the first man gurgled, wet sounds coming from the falling guard's gaping neck before I could gather a breath to scream. The other gasped, burbling, chest erupting with blood as Charlotte jerked her hand free and let him fall at her feet.

"Charlotte!" It came out in a choking whisper, horror washing over me as my fingers touched the wetness on my skin. Came back smeared red.

Her muzzle shrank slightly, but her half-wolf form remained.

"You want me to let them kill you?" Her voice wasn't her voice any more, rough and unkempt, deep as an endless night, full of the howl of the wild. "It's time you understood how serious this is, Syd."

I'd never seen her kill before. Lived in this happy bubble of ignorance. Yes, people died around me. But never thanks to my side. Why did it shock me so much she was capable of such violence?

Wow. Just. Wow.

She lifted her face, wolf-muzzle returning. "This way," she growled.

I followed, Demetrius happily humming beside me, an abrupt and forced shift in thinking going on in my head. Charlotte was a killer. She just killed those two sorcerers. Yes, they'd killed witches. Yes, they'd burned them and crushed their bones.

But Charlotte killed. And she did it for me.

So innocent, so childish, Syd. And yet...

Could I live with this?

I shook myself as we passed under more dim lighting, night-time illumination casting the halls in shadow. The thick carpet under my feet turned to marble as we stepped out into a grand lobby, three large elevator doors on the left, another big desk on the right. But the place was silent, still. No guards, no more Brotherhood.

"They knew we'd take the stairs." I followed after Charlotte while Demetrius's song went quiet.

"No," he said. "They don't know we're coming." His blue eyes glowed eerily in the low light. "Or we would never have made it past the lobby door."

Okay then.

Happy thoughts.

I glanced to the right, at the elaborate sign and logo hanging over the reception desk. Coterie Industries sprawled across the wall, a C and I interlaced with a globe.

I'd have to dig out a dictionary later, but I was pretty sure "coterie" was just another way to say "brotherhood".

As we passed through the lobby and down another hall, padding past elaborate office doors, a glass boardroom overlooking the city and the ocean, I realized just how clever the Brotherhood was. An international corporation would give them access to anything they needed. Unlike witches and most other magical races who kept to themselves as a protective measure, the sorcerer's league seemed to have taken advantage of the world of the normals.

"They control massive amounts of technology," Demetrius said, his lucidity with us again. "Bio-tech, weapons, software, genetic manipulation."

Quaid grunted, arm still around his sister. "I've heard of them," he said. "They spearheaded a new genetically enhanced crop placement in Africa. Some kind of grain that thrives without much water."

Demetrius turned and stared up into Quaid's eyes as we all stopped, even Charlotte, while the little man's body vibrated in rage.

"They have been positioning themselves for centuries," he said. "This new age of technology has given them their first chance to take over everything." His blue eyes met mine. "And they have, Sydlynn. They have taken everything." He shuddered, giggled, physically pulled himself back under control. How much effort did it take him to come back to us? "The grain Quaid talks about will enslave everyone who eats it. Slowly, over time. They've already begun testing on normals on this continent, in Europe. But the crop they are sending to Africa will be their first real attempt to take over a population."

Un. Freaking. Believable. "The normals have no idea."

"How could they?" Demetrius quivered, lips

wobbling, a hysterical whine escaping him as he finally lost control. "They already ate their souls!" He laughed out loud, so loud Charlotte pounced on him, one half-wolf hand firmly pressing over his mouth as he fought her, blue eyes full of the agony of one trapped in madness. He finally stilled and she released him. Demetrius crouched down, panting, shaking his head. "They will use them against us," he whispered in a hoarse voice. "And we won't stand a chance."

Not if I had something to say about it.

We moved on, Demetrius hugging himself, muttering under his breath. I needed him focused, but when I reached to touch his arm he jerked away from me with a snarl and bared teeth.

Fine, I'd manage on my own. But he'd better snap the hell out of it when the time came.

I glanced sideways at a large door, partially open, a gold plaque mounted at eye level. My eyes drifted away only to flash back as I stopped in my tracks to stare.

Liander Belaisle.

CEO.

Oh. My. Swearword.

The leader of the Brotherhood—the man I'd fought and defeated, who Trill, Owen and I chased off, was the CEO of the whole shebang. Not some petty lieutenant as I assumed, but the head honcho.

I wondered if cutting off his head would kill this

particular snake.

My stomach flipped over slowly. As often as I joked with myself about killing, now that the blood of the enemy was on me, it didn't seem like such a great thing to joke about. Quaid had warned me, when I stood over Ameline in the cave, when she struggled with the three Sidhe souls inside her, actually killing someone would change me.

I now had no doubt he was right.

And yet. Liander Belaisle was the enemy. And had no qualms about killing.

Which meant I had to get over my little princess fit and fast.

The end of the corridor beckoned, a glowing red EXIT sign over a wooden door.

Demetrius stopped in front of it, looked at me.

"The roof," he said. "The machine."

Bring it.

Chapter Twenty Seven

It wasn't like I expected a cake walk or anything. But it would have been nice if we could have just strolled through the exit door, climbed the short staircase to the roof, sauntered up to the machine of doom and broken it into a million pieces while kindly handing Mia's power back, safe and sound.

Um hum. Dream time over in three, two, one—

I might have done all right against a heavy bag Sage had me working with at the gym, but taking on giant sorcerers in expensive suits was another matter altogether. The second we passed through the roof door and into the narrow stairwell to the top, three of them rushed out, one falling with a cry as Demetrius, more prepared than I was, took him out at the knees with a slash of his crystal. I didn't think the stone itself did the damage. But whatever Demetrius's power did to the big guard, he crashed forward, almost taking out Quaid as he fell, a redwood crashing in the forest. Charlotte's claws liberated another of his life, more blood spraying outward in an arc of red as the sorcerer's throat opened in three deep slashes.

Taking Demetrius's lead, I struck with my own crystal, my meager protective learning enough, thanks to the pressure of my other powers. My demon's fire, now tied to my sorcery, seared the guard's face, sending him stumbling back, hands raised in protection while Shaylee reached beneath me and buckled the floor. A long rattling ended in a screech as marble cracked, steel girders puncturing the heavy stone as the very floor crushed its way upward. Sharp metal teeth, jagged and smoking from the vast pressure the earth magic applied, split the door entry in two, the frame collapsing to one side, landing on Demetrius's victim with crushing results.

So much blood.

If I hadn't been deep in my magic, I know I would have puked.

Demetrius didn't wait to see if more hulking bodies in suits waited for us, but rushed through, hopping over the wreck of the floor and the bleeding body of Charlotte's victim, disappearing up the stairs. I followed at a dead run, the whole world in sharp relief, everything brilliantly clear as adrenaline tightened my focus. I felt my heart beating, heard my breath. Caught the scent of the ocean again on the other side of the coppery smell of blood. Gasped at the rush of heat as Demetrius threw open the narrow, metal door at the top of the steps and vanished into the night.

Cold air full of death reclaimed the space as the door thudded shut. I didn't hesitate, keeping myself tightly inside this new feeling of attention, silently thanking Quaid for the exercises I'd practiced, knowing this hyper-awareness came from the combination of adrenaline and confidence. Two leaps of two steps at a time and I jerked the door open, flying through it into the humid Miami night.

Ready for a fight, burning for it.

But none came. I caught a glimpse of movement ahead, spotted Demetrius running the length of the building and raced after him. Charlotte chuffed next to me as she morphed further into wolf form, loping at my side on four legs. A silver streak of fur raced past her, heading for Demetrius as I wondered what Sassafras thought he could accomplish without power.

I glanced over my shoulder, saw Quaid, Mia in his arms, running after us. This time I supplied him magic support and he nodded grimly in thanks.

The rooftop was empty, all but for some outtakes of air conditioning, the giant units roaring into the darkness, and a sculpture on the far end, facing inland. I slid to a halt on the pebbled asphalt roof, the stink of it rising to assault me, heat making the footing sticky. Demetrius pointed as I tried to make sense of what I saw.

Five pillars, taller than me, taller than the goon squad we'd taken out, stood in a rough circle around another central column. No ordinary pillars. My sorcery called to them as I approached, the pulse of their magic warming to greet the stone in my hand.

Crystals. But not the rough edged ones I was used to. These hulked their way skyward, polished columns, each glowing softly from within with their own subtle beauty, facets clearly visible past surfaces as smooth as glass. All the colors of magic pulsed here: green, white, red, blue, amber. I circled them slowly, eyes going to the ground, realizing then this was no circle.

They stood at the points of the pentagram, and the central crystal, its heart black and opaque, loomed in the middle. The Brotherhood used the power of the covens, the same pattern we called on to reinforce our family magic, to connect and bind us together.

Learned a thing or two from us, it seemed.

"This," Demetrius's lower lip quivered as he came to stand beside me, shoulders sagging, tears welling in his eyes. "Monstrous."

I reached for it with power, feeling each of the columns answer me, wake, hum to life.

Try to feed from me.

My vampire snarled, demon howling her fury while

Shaylee's earth magic made the rooftop rumble. I slammed up shields against the crystals as they seemed to sigh in sadness before falling still again.

But no. Not still. Not quite. They were still drawing on power, weren't they? I could feel the subtle thread they pulled toward them, closed my eyes a moment before opening them slowly. Yes. There. The threads were real, barely visible to my magic sight. Sucking in power.

From everywhere. Multiple trails, from hundreds of sources, flooding the columns with energy.All of it, every scrap, funneling through them into the center of the pentagram, to the heart of darkness waiting.

To the black stone, the one in the middle. Silent as death, absorbing power as though it ate the light.

"We must shatter the crystals." Demetrius jabbed at me with one sharp finger. "They've taken enough power the machine does its work for them."

I stared at him. "The Dumont magic," I said. It now made complete, horrible sense. How would we end, I wondered, standing there, staring at the possibility of the end of magic? Would it build, this drawing of power, until, like the crack in a dam, it burst, and we lost all of our power in one great wave? Or, would it go on like this, subtle and slow, the loss so incremental we didn't notice until it was too late? Until all of the magic was eaten alive?

Demetrius's head bobbed, hair waving around his damaged cherub face. "It's awake now," he said. "It has a soul. And it must feed."

Quaid stopped behind me, the press of his shoulder against my back sticking my t-shirt to my slick skin. But I welcomed the contact, didn't feel the heat anymore, not through the chill of discovery.

"This is why they haven't bothered to attack anyone else," he said. "They don't have to, do they, Demetrius?"

The little man sighed sadly. "No," he said, singing the words. "Not now. It will eat and eat until nothing is left but what they own. Just like the rest of their plans."

"How do we stop it, Demetrius?" A part of me felt guilty, imagine. But the pulsing soul of the crystal in my hand felt so similar to the heartbeats I'd felt in the large columns I wondered what I'd done, if the crystal I had in my possession was as dangerous as the magic siphon before me. "How do we destroy it?"

He turned and looked up at me from the corner of his eye, hand reaching for mine, holding it like a little kid who needed his mommy to save him. "There's only one way," he said. "Maji."

The power of creation. That didn't make any sense. "How can I create them into destroying themselves?" Damn it, I knew so little, really about what I was. About what I could do. A little appearance from my maji guardian/teacher/pain in my ass, Iepa, would have been pretty helpful right about then.

Like that was going to happen.

Sydlynn, my vampire sent. *We've already had this conversation.*

We had?

Creation magic not only creates, it controls. She sounded a little miffed I'd forgotten. *All other magicks bow to it, can be manipulated and altered by it. It is literally the reason for other magic.*

Oh yeah. I seemed to recall she mentioned that to me when we fought Quaid, after the Seelie Queen Aiolainn thralled him.

What had my vampires said then? *Creation magic controlled all other magicks.* That was the true power of the maji.

Gotcha, I sent. Creation magic it was.

Charlotte's scream turned me half-way around, just as the crack of a whip jarred my ears. I saw her flying toward me, her half wolf form filling out, eyes wide and wolfish. But I wasn't paying attention to her, not really, not when something slammed into me, shoving me back, stumbling, falling.

Shoulder on fire as I went down.

chapter twenty eight

Slow.

Motion.

I heard Charlotte howling, drawn out and garbled, as I fell back, the unexpected blow bending my knees, dropping me like a rock to the stinking rooftop. My head struck the surface, bounced from the asphalt as the burning in my shoulder grew in intensity, from flames to a raging inferno.

My vampire hissed in my head, spirit magic surging even as my demon roared her rage. I struggled to sit up, hand clenching around my crystal despite the raging pain racing down my arm, my demon driving me to act, to protect myself, while the ball of fire erupted in agony, gasp worthy pain racing across my chest and down my arm, blooming in time with my heartbeat. I rolled on my side as Quaid sank to his haunches next to me, face crumpled in fear, hands reaching for me. So fast, it all happened so fast, so slow. I turned to Charlotte, in wolf form, as she leaped between me and the advancing line of dark-suited men, the one in the front pointing something at me.

At her.

Another crack of the whip. Charlotte's high-pitched yelp of canine agony drove me to my knees. I shoved Quaid aside with the shoulder that wasn't on fire, my power lunging for my bodywere as she crumpled and fell to the rooftop.

Human again as she crashed to the ground.

Fell still.

I pressed one hand to my shoulder as time came back to normal, cried out at the pain my touch caused, pulled away to find my fingers and palm slick with blood. Liander Belaisle came to a grinning halt next to Charlotte, the gun in his hand still trailing smoke from the end of the barrel.

He shot me?

Seriously?

Rage surged, my demon taking over, vampire pouring more spirit magic over the bullet hole even as I lashed out with a whip of my own, slashing across the line of sorcerers who came to challenge me.

My power died against a wall of nothing, pattering to the ground in a sheet of sparks.

More guns, more grins. All the confidence in the world.

Belaisle prodded Charlotte with one shiny shoe, towering over her quiet body though she was taller than him standing, looking down at her like he owned her. Terror clenched in my gut when she didn't move, twitch. Breathe. A large pool of wetness spread beneath her, shining in the highest lights of the city reflecting onto the rooftop.

I had to save her! My feet wouldn't support me, knees weak with fear, my power reaching for Charlotte, desperate, so desperate.

Only to find her trapped on the other side of Belaisle's control.

The wall of empty kept me from her. I gasped her name, knowing I had no time to reach her physically, to save her. Not now. Maybe not ever.

Not when Belaisle turned the muzzle of his pistol and pointed it at Quaid.

Oh no, he did *not*.

Sydlynn, my vampire's screech bit through my shock. *The weapon.*

Yes. Yes, of course. This time I didn't attack the man, but his machine. He might be behind the shielding, but he foolishly allowed his gun to pass through the front edge and left it vulnerable. The black flower beneath me bloomed open, welcoming me, begging to be fed, and I obliged. The wall of empty shielding suctioned around the barrel pulled me, like magic to like until it wasn't empty anymore.

I felt Belaisle shift, his finger tightening on the trigger, touched the gun with my sorcery, used it to fight back. Poured all of my rage and hate and need to punish him into the metal in his bare hand.

Belaisle cried out in pain and fury as the gun flared red hot. He tossed it aside, smoking, turning to glare at me.

Before grinning again. And pulling back one foot and planting it in Charlotte's stomach.

She lifted from the roof at least a half foot, body flipping over before landing hard, the motion rolling her over onto her back. Her head fell to one side, face upturned toward me. A mess of black liquid coated her chest, stained her skimpy underwear, red glints showing in what light we had.

But it was her empty eyes I found myself lost in.

"You and your magic," Belaisle said as I choked on grief, consuming sadness, knowing she was—no. I couldn't think that. There had to be hope. She was playing, biding her time. Letting Belaisle think he'd beaten her. Any moment now she'd rise, fight back—

He adjusted the front of his tailored suit, worried about appearances while my bodywere—my friend—continued to bleed on the filthy rooftop. His fingers brushed over the small goatee on his chin as I turned slowly back to him, letting the grief spin into a tornado of hate fueling my power. "You forget there are other means, Miss Hayle. Much more effective." He strode past Charlotte's quiet form while I shook inside, grief still fighting, though my rage won for now as my demon, vampire and Sidhe princess fought to keep me level.

Level. What good balance when Charlotte was—

"I'm not certain mere bullets will be able to kill you at this point," the blood had already stopped flowing from my shoulder as my vampire did her work, "thanks to what you're becoming." He stopped a few feet away, hands sliding into his trouser pockets. "Yes, my dear, I know exactly what you're becoming." Bastard.

Charlotte was right.

Killing was the only option.

But Charlotte was—

"Bullets will, however, kill your friends." Belaisle gestured behind him. The sound of guns cocking froze me in place.

I should never have brought them with me.

Never.

Belaisle's gaze fell on Demetrius and, for the first time, a flash of real anger crossed his face.

"I should have put you out of your misery the last time we met, Strong." Belaisle's voice lost the silky polish of polite society, a more common accent, something rough and almost backwoods, tainting his speech.

Poser. I knew it.

Demetrius stuck out his tongue, thumbs in his ears, waggling his fingers at the Brotherhood leader. "Sticks and stones, Andy," he said.

Would have been funny.

If not for Charlotte—

Wasn't.

"Well then," Belaisle said. "I'll just have to correct that mistake, won't I?" He half-turned, calling over his shoulder. "Bring my crystal. I'll drain him first. And a new gun."

"They know about you now," I said, spit out around the knowledge Charlotte wasn't getting up again. Belaisle ignored me, turned as one of the Brotherhood stepped forward, placing a cloth bag in one of his leader's hands and a dull black pistol in the other. But I kept going anyway, babbling, furious.

Heartbroken.

"The Enforcers will find you and destroy this machine." I wished I believed it.

Belaisle laughed as he slid the crystal from the bag, holding it in his left hand while he balanced the new gun in his right. He took his time, still standing confidently behind his wall of protection, gun and all. Too bad he wasn't about to make the same mistake twice. I could feel it better now, his shielding, thanks to my own sorcery. He called on the ranks of sorcerers he brought with him, almost blotting himself out from magical view so much power poured into it. "How foolish and romantic and utterly ridiculous." He pointed the crystal at Demetrius. "Tell her, Strong. Tell her no one will come."

Demetrius whined softly, looked away.

Yeah, I wasn't holding out hope either. And I was now out of threats.

Your maji power is all we have left, my vampire sent.

He'll kill them, I sent back with my soul collapsing inside me, my eyes settling on Charlotte—

Stop it. My vampire's power slapped me, hard. *We can't think about her now, Syd. Even if it means they die. That we die. We have to stop Belaisle.*

I squeezed the crystal in my hand, the pain of the sharp edges digging in. Pain brought clarity, even as the wakened crystal fed the dark flower beneath me. It continued to gape open, welcoming me. But it wasn't alone. I had them all now, all magicks, access to more than enough. And thanks to the blood staining my skin, I had the final trigger to waken my creation magic.

Rage ruling me, all of my magicks begging to be freed, I called on the maji.

Felt my power come together.

Just as Demetrius howled in rage and leaped for Belaisle.

chapter twenty nine

The leader of the Brotherhood didn't get a chance to pull the trigger. And neither did Demetrius make it to his destination. An outward blast of power sent me flying back, Quaid and Mia next to me, Demetrius falling in my lap as I landed hard between two of the towering crystal columns.

We weren't the only ones. Sorcerers went tumbling like ten pins as a giant, black hole opened in the center of the roof, gushing iridescent light around the edges. Belaisle's lips moved as though he cursed, but the sound was lost in the roar of wind as three figures stepped out of the black hole just before it crushed itself out of existence.

Trill stood in the center of the gap, long hair settling around her, arms dropping to her sides as she released her power. Owen stood next to her, gaping mouth and eyes no longer endless pits of darkness. The pair clearly mastered their abilities, tied them together even, but not without help. A third form stood between them, blackness and light all wound together around him. Hope rose in me again, even as my friend's companion, a tall, handsome guy it turned out when his own magic faded, offered Liander a wave and a smile.

"Long time no see." He turned and winked at me, eyes as blue as Owen's. "You're welcome."

I'd be pissed about his attitude later. Belaisle and his people pulled themselves to their feet, and together, advanced while Belaisle glared at the trio. I stood, too, trying to find my maji again.

Only to realize everything was gone. My head was silent. My right hand closed reflexively around the crystal.

The crystal that wasn't there anymore.

Damn, how had I lost it? Dropped it in the arrival of the Zornovs.

Helpless. Hopeless.

I had to find it.

Belaisle wasn't about to wait for me to scramble around searching for my crystal. He raised his gun and pointed it at Trill.

Pulled the trigger.

I screamed, a sob punching me in the chest, seeing Charlotte, knowing another of my friends gave her life.

Only to gape as the bullet slowed. Stopped. Came to

hover in front of Trill. She plucked it gently from the air, let it sit in her palm. Blew on it. The metal burst into sparks and dispersed under her breath.

"You'll have to do better than that," she said.

Hell, *yes*!

Syd. Trill's mental voice reached me. But how? It wasn't until I saw Owen's hand in hers I understood. She used his sorcery to touch mine. *I'll handle Belaisle. Destroy that machine.*

I spun to look for my crystal, knowing she was right, only to have Demetrius grab my hand and pull me forward, into the circle. Toward the big black column.

I showed him my empty hands, tried to turn away and find what I'd lost, but he tugged against me as the air behind me burst into rapid gun fire. I had to go back, to help my friends! Something pinged from one of the crystal columns, a sharp slice across my cheek stinging as a shard cut me.

We weren't alone, then, Quaid dragging Mia into the center with us, ducking behind one of the columns. His dark eyes met mine, fear as real as his resolve.

Demetrius pinched me to gain my attention, scowling. "Focus," he said. "Here, you see?" He held up his crystal, showed me the lines running through it. Someone screamed, a man's scream. I couldn't focus, what was he thinking? How could I possibly pay attention while there was a good chance those I cared about were likely dying?

To buy me time.

Suck it the hell up and get to work, Hayle.

Right.

I looked, drew a breath, fought for calm.

"Here," he said, pointing with one very grubby finger. "You see it?"

At first I didn't. Low light, no way to augment my vision, distractions pulling at me. But just as I was about to shake my head, the glint of illumination when he turned the crystal showed me what he pointed to.

A flaw. Deep inside.

"Fragile," he whispered. Gestured around him at the columns. "Only as strong as their weakest point." He leaned forward and pounded on the outside of the black one. "No way to do it from here," he said. "But from inside..." He pinched me again. "Inside is weak."

Inside. "You want me to go inside the crystal?" Seriously, there was only so much I could take. This wasn't the Node, all soft and liquid. It was a solid piece of stone.

"Not you," he snarled. Poked me between the eyes. "*You.*"

He was making no sense and I was out of patience. "Just freaking show me," I snarled.

"No!" Mia lunged to her feet, leaving Quaid's side. I turned, distracted, realizing the sound of gunshots had faded to one or two at a time, flashes of light and guttering black just visible past the crystals. "Let me!"

She pushed me aside, hugging the black stone, weeping as she lay against it. Quaid rushed forward, but I held him back as Mia leaned away, blue eyes closed in concentration.

"My life," she said, "my magic. Come to me."

The crystal pulsed, once. I almost thought I imagined it before it pulsed again, a lavender rim forming around the edges. She was doing it. Calling out the family magic. Even Demetrius gaped as though he didn't think she could do it.

A hysterical laugh built in my chest as Mia's lips spread in a smile, arms wide open to welcome her family magic home.

"Mia?"

We all stopped, stared as a tall, broad-shouldered figure emerged from the back side of the machine. Mia turned, arms dropping, expression crumpling as Rupe entered the light. His smile was small, secret, face open. One hand reached for her even as Quaid snarled under his breath.

"Blood." Mia sighed out his old Goth name and my hope cracked down the middle.

Quaid eased around me, heading for Rupe, but I knew he was too late.

"I'm sorry," Rupe said. "They made me lead them to you. This was all a mistake." Mia nodded, leaning toward him even as the rippling lavender fire retreated back into the crystal. Quaid was almost in position, hate burning in his eyes. But he didn't stand a chance, not when Rupe took one more step toward Mia and smiled. "You know I love you."

She rushed to him, falling into Rupe's arms just before Quaid reached them. A heavy thrum of empty magic hit my chest as Quaid flew backward, impacting one of the crystals, falling, unconscious on his side.

Mia screamed, thin and wailing, turning to claw at Rupe's chest. The sound of his fist hitting her jaw hurt me even from a distance. She went silent with a squeak, spinning sideways before tumbling to the rooftop.

I met Rupe's eyes with hate of my own even as he saluted me.

"I really have to thank you, Syd," he said, laughter in his voice. "If it wasn't for you, I never would have found out I was a sorcerer."

And I'd called him my friend, once. Trusted him. "You're welcome," I snarled. "Too bad you won't live long enough to enjoy it."

Shouting, renewed gunfire, echoed from the other side of the crystals. Trill had to be holding her own. But I had no idea how long she would last. My eyes went to her direction. Caught sight of a ball of silver fluff. Amber eyes winked at me before Sassafras turned and ran away.

For help. Just like he promised.

If he made it.

I turned back to the black column, knowing our only hope lay there now. Rupe took a step toward me, but Demetrius hissed and slashed at him with his own sorcery, the footing under Rupe's feet giving way, sending him tumbling back with a cry.

"Now," Demetrius said, grabbing my hand, forcing his crystal into it, squeezing our flesh together over the sharp stone. "Inside."

I followed where he led, felt myself lift free of my body. The urge to fight was so powerful, to return to my mortal form, I almost ruined everything. But they saved me.

Surrounding me, outside me as I was outside myself. My vampire, my demon, my Sidhe princess. Freed as I was freed.

Together, we followed Demetrius into the heart of darkness.

chapter thirty

So black, so thick, the world was gone. And then light, thin and distorted, tinted deep purple, all around me. My vampire stood beside me, her white power flaring, stained by the crystal's heart. My demon and Shaylee both stayed close, back to back with me, a four-cornered star as we all peered outward into the dark.

A shining light appeared on my left, floating toward me. When he came close enough to recognize, Demetrius's smile lit my heart, blue eyes as clear as any crystal, no sign of the insanity in control of his mind, the damage to his body not visible on him here. In this place.

In the center of the heart of darkness.

I felt it then, the subtle hum of it, the pull of magic feeding it. Felt it try to devour me, a slow and lazy suction until I showed it the flower of sorcery at my base, the black of its petals a perfect match for the crystal. With a surge of joy it welcomed me, reversed its process, now supplying me with power, siphoning it back into my various magicks, as though I required nourishment. My soul shriveled even as I allowed the feeding. Not because I craved the power. But because doing so allowed me control over the stone.

How much, I didn't know. But as long as it didn't try to hurt me, thought of me as part of it, I would do everything I could to keep it happy until I found the means to destroy it.

And yet, my mind, freed from my physical body, from the worries of the outside world, felt the heart of the crystal and knew the truth. Evil didn't live here, not at all. The stone had a soul, clear of judgment, open and trusting. Seeking power only because doing so was its nature.

Joy came from purpose. Happiness was fulfilling that purpose.

Siphoning magic. And keeping it safe.

We must act together, Demetrius sent. I could only guess he felt unaffected by the heart of the stone while my empathy grew for it moment by moment. How could I destroy something so precious, life, beautiful life, a soul without darkness despite its purpose?

My vampire prodded me, the bite of spirit magic bringing me back to myself. *All of us*. My vampire nodded to him, demon snarling even as Shaylee squeezed my hand. I shuddered, knowing how close I'd come to falling into the stone's need. My vampire went on without me. *If we work in tandem, we can use the power contained in this place to fracture its heart.*

Something flashed past the periphery of my vision, on the other side of the crystal. I could just make out shapes moving around and felt fear for my friends rise.

Trust them to give us the time we need, Demetrius sent. Offered his hand. *This is our only hope.*

He was right. I knew it. Didn't help much.

Search for the seams. I already knew what to look for, had seen the tiny cracks in the heart of his crystal. *They will be here, but well hidden. We must find one of its flaws before we can act.*

Did the crystal sense our intent? If so, it did nothing to act against us. Instead, it called to me again, tried to embrace me, a beloved child, a kindred spirit it longed to share its purpose with. Guilt returned as I searched for the means to destroy it. So beautiful in here, so quiet and perfect, all sharp edges and flawless motion and, ever increasing, power. All the power I would ever need. As simple as accepting my task.

Opening the last of my will to the dark.

Perfect.

Sydlynn. My vampire's power bit so deep this time I cried out and jerked free of her. My mind swirled with conflict, though I grasped at her in thanks for again shaking me free of the lure of the crystal.

Here. She drew me closer to center, down deep, near the base of the column, coming with me this time as the lure pulled at my sorcery. *You feel it.*

I did. The hairline crack was barely a crack at all, a tiny flaw in the stone. But Demetrius seized on the fissure, his power flowing through our held hands and into me.

Press here, he sent. I hesitated, bloom of sorcery begging me to feed it. But my vampire held me with her, my demon and Shaylee gathering near, their power holding me with them.

I pressed where Demetrius told me to. Against the edge of the crack. It did nothing at first, as unyeilding as any stone. But I could sense the breaking point. If I could just find it...

A sharp retort echoed around me, through me, and I screamed from the pain even as the crystal screamed. Demetrius's hold on my hand, my vampire on the other, pulled me back.

You link too close, Demetrius sent. *And yet, that is the only way we can defeat it.*

By linking with the heart of the stone.

It might kill her, my vampire sent. Oddly calm when she said it as though such a loss would be acceptable.

I had to agree.

It might. Demetrius sighed. *There is no recourse.*

Agreed. My vampire let me go. My demon rumbled, but nodded. And Shaylee bowed her head, turning away.

Life and death, huh? Hadn't been here before or anything. And though I knew my alter egos worried, I didn't. As I allowed myself to sink back into the soul of the crystal, I was very sure I'd survive.

I just wasn't sure I could follow through with destroying the heart.

The crystal welcomed me as before, guileless, as naïve as Liander accused me of being. It opened to me as I whispered to it, joined with it, let it pull me in the rest of the way.

It was only then the Dumont family magic appeared, rising from the core, winding around me, tense and unhappy. It could probably still feel Mia on the other side. But despite the unrest of the power it held, the black column's calm and deep joy never changed.

Purpose was everything.

Unknowing, the Dumont power gave me the edge I needed to break the hold of the call to feed.

Smaller clumps of power slid around me now, crying piteously, tiny seeds of families long gone. I sank deeper, anchoring to the Dumont power, my sorcery's flower opening, petals gaping wide, mouth of blackness calling me home. For the first time, I let my sorcery have its way without holding back, absorbed the taint of it, the destructive magic of using one thing's power for another thing's gain. Unlike witchcraft, demon magic, even Sidhe power, sorcery was based in the utter obliteration of the source of its magic.

No wonder the Brotherhood were a dark and terrible league. I could feel my soul shrivel at the touch of the gaping wound that was my sorcery. The aching hunger rising from it, the need to feed and feed in order to survive. I'd starved it my entire life, as I'd starved my other magicks, at least until I was sixteen. But my sorcery had only woken recently. And its desperate need to swell and grow scared the crap out of me.

I needed it too, though, didn't I? As much as my other sources of power.

For the first time since I found out where my evolution was heading, I worried about what the end result really might look like.

No time for selfishness. The flaw sat before me, widened, but still small. I wormed my way inside it even as my sorcery begged to devour the Dumont power swirling around me, to gobble the other tiny magicks like snacks. I instead showed it the ultimate feast, used the black to seep through the gap, oozing into the micro fracture, pointed my power in the right direction until it saw.

And understood.

My sorcery didn't hesitate when it found its prize. Acted while I shuddered and backed away, letting it do what it wanted, wished things were different. It drew on the strength of the column, pulling not at the stored magic, but the inherent power built into the stone itself.

The black flower gulped energy, petals swelling, eager and grasping. I screamed silently into the depth of the stone as my sorcery devoured it, eating its heart, swallowing its soul, weakening it until it sighed and sagged around me. The sad song of the crystal made me weep, heart aching for what I'd become. But I had no choice.

No choice at all.

The Dumont power rose around me as the stone died, Mia's family magic clinging to me for safety while I swam to the surface. Cracks appeared, sharp and jagged, endless snapping and popping making my head ache. The smaller pockets of magic circled us, the voices of their hope rising, drowning out the last of the crystal's song as it finally sighed one last note and died.

Demetrius was with me, my egos, all of us together, the Dumont family magic and that of the other covens pulled tight as the small sorcerer nodded sharply to me.

Now, he sent.

I focused all of my power on the central crack and pushed.

chapter thirty one

The world fragmented around me, slicing crystals bursting with explosive force. I flowed with them, from them, slamming into my body, the force of four souls coming together rocking my physical form even as I raised my arms and threw up my shields.

Liander thought bullets were efficient. Flying shards of crystal would do the job just as well.

Only problem, I had terrible aim.

A crystal shard whispered past my ear before freezing in place, much as Trill's bullet had, my shielding catching the flying projectiles and then releasing them all at once to tinkle harmlessly to the ground. I would have loved to let them fly, but I had no way of knowing if they would take out friend or foe and I just couldn't risk it.

The building below me groaned as though in agony as the power inside the black column vanished, the entire structure suffering from the loss. The feeling of my other egos remained with me, my magic intact, the petals of the dark flower at my base sighing shut, sated for now on the power of the dead crystal.

It was only when my magic pulsed, unfettered, I realized the protections around Brotherhood territory shattered with the crystal I destroyed.

"No!" I spun to find Belaisle pushing his way past the red pillar, heading for me. He seemed ready to lunge, attack me physically before he stopped, staring, hate and rage and fear on his face.

Time to show him who was really in control here. I raised my hand, my power reaching inside the crystal beside him. I knew what to look for now, found it easily. Welcomed the flower to open once more. Used the stored magic inside my sorcery to access all the flaws deep inside the pillar. And as I closed my hand into a fist, the column imploded, red fire shooting upward from its core, lost in the night sky.

Belaisle fell to one side, shouting an incoherent curse as I reached for the next one, amber demon magic escaping as I crushed that column, too. An amazing and terrible joy surged inside me at their destruction, calling on me to do more damage, to draw out more power.

The loss of the two towering pillars exposed part of the rooftop to my view, the crumpled forms of suited Brotherhood sorcerers scattered across its dark surface, only a handful remaining behind Belaisle while Trill, Owen and their companion stared at me, a swirling maelstrom of black and white magic falling to pool at their feet.

I held Belaisle's eyes as I shattered the forth column, heard the song of the Sidhe echo in the air, felt its rumble under my feet as the fifth collapsed, vampire's hiss swooping over my head before vanishing.

The sixth and last fell behind me, the pull of the witch magic embedded in it so strong I almost allowed it to join me, before sending it on its way, a wild trail of blue tracing a track across the dark sky until it, too, disappeared.

It was hard, so very hard, to force the dark flower to close again. It longed for Belaisle and his people, hungry for the power they held, trying to feast on them.

I almost let it.

Almost.

Belaisle's glare of fury turned to fear as my sorcery's swollen desires fell on him. But as I soothed the power to stillness, he slowly relaxed, settling finally into his familiar smile, though, from the tightness around his eyes, he wasn't as good an actor as he believed.

"You fool," he said. "I would have devoured you."

"There's still time," I snarled. "Patience."

He fell back a step, smile faltering. "This was merely one piece of the puzzle." His fists thudded against his thighs as he spoke, betraying his continued fury. "We have many more in play and you can't possibly find them all."

I shrugged, smiled back, let him feel my smug happiness. All those threats, what lay still uncovered? For tomorrow. I beat his ass. Time to rub his nasty face in it.

"We'll see," I said. "Now, are you going to come quietly, or do I have to knock the crap out of you first?"

He didn't get to answer. The air around me burst with magic, flares of blue followed by small rushes of wind as a floating army of Enforcers appeared overhead. Belaisle took one look at them and snarled before snapping his fingers at his men.

As one, they turned and ran, the Enforcers swooping after them. Only one remained behind, a tall, blonde man tucked against one side, a silver Persian held to the other. Sassafras leaped free from Pender Tremere's arms and raced to me, a streak of light, before launching himself into my arms.

I held him tucked close, his purr giving me focus as I stared at Andre.

I had to, Sass sent, mental voice full of misery. *Forgive me, but Andre is the only choice, now.*

I forgot Sass watched Mia crumble under Rupe's influence. Looked around to find the traitorous ex-Goth gone, run off with Belaisle, no doubt. Only then did I remember at last why we'd come here. Spotted Mia leaning against Quaid, both staring at Andre Dumont. The swirling mass of the Dumont family magic sighed as it hovered next to me, spinning slowly, sullen and rumbling, still clinging for support. The tiny pockets of magic circling it came to hover at my feet as Andre stepped forward, eyes locked on the power using me for shelter.

Mia lurched to standing, glaring at the male Dumont. "What are you doing here?"

He sneered, smoothing back his blonde hair, all nicely put together while Mia looked like she'd been dragged through something unsavory. And, to her credit, she had.

There was still a chance for her, no matter what Sass thought.

Mia, I sent. *Reach for the magic. Don't hesitate.*

She spun on me, eyes wide and staring.

This is your fault, she hissed back before turning to the family power and again raising her arms, opening them wide to the power she once possessed.

"Come to me!" She shook with need, taking a step closer. But even before Andre spoke I felt it.

Resistance. Punishment. Anger.

Loathing because she'd been unable to save it.

Andre's smooth voice, his soft French accent lilting and alluring, broke over Mia's. "Come to me."

The lavender tornado sped up. Didn't hesitate.

Dove directly for Andre and slammed full-force into

his chest.

And the first male leader of a coven was created while the old one screamed her denial.

Chapter Thirty Two

There was nothing left for me to do. Not while Andre swelled with power and Mia sagged, sobbing into her hands. While I hadn't done it personally, I had a hand in my friend's ruin.

Sorrow washed through me as I turned, met Quaid's eyes. Saw his grief for his sister. Glanced over his shoulder.

And sobbed myself, once. She lay crumpled on her side, bare skin pale, blonde hair spread around her, stained dark with her blood. Charlotte's stillness told me what I needed to know, but I went to her anyway. To confront her loss.

Sassafras jumped down, approaching her face. Touched her nose with his small, pink one. Jerked back and hissed as he looked up at me. "Syd," he said. "She's still warm."

Impossible. I fell to my knees, my power reaching for Charlotte. But she was gone, no heartbeat, no breath. And yet, he was right.

She hadn't died from the bullet wound after all.

Charlotte survived all this time only to die just before I reached her.

Heaving sobs ripped me open as I fell over her, pulling her to me, cradling her in my lap. I dove inside her with my power, refusing to accept her loss, reaching for her, pulling, pushing even as my vampire dove deeper still.

Like this, Gram sent, flooding my mind with her power, the tang of her necromancy searing through my body. Illegal, but I didn't care about the rules.

Not when it came to saving Charlotte's life.

Gram's power flared. Softened. Fell away as the emptiness stretched on and on forever.

I'm sorry, she whispered at last.

The thread of who Charlotte was had broken. Her soul was gone.

No.

It couldn't have gone far, though, could it?

Not far enough.

The maji in me whispered, sang a song of rejuvenation, pulled me along, further than Gram had taken me, deeper still. All the way to the black wall, to the glow of light that was the only flaw in its perfect darkness.

I found her there, almost through. Pulled her back, drew her from the dark place, from the calling light where she hovered, staring, her soul and her echo, the ghost of what would remain locked together in an embrace. When I called for her, when my maji power reached her, Charlotte's soul turned, so innocent, her face bright and happy while her echo's expression turned to grief as the wolf rose and took over her ghost.

Will you let me go? Happy Charlotte looked at the light.

I will, I said, though everything in me fought her choice. *If you choose to leave us.*

Her echo held tighter, snarling, the wolf refusing to release her. *I'm not ready.* She turned to me, grasped for me, ghostly paw curved into claws that bit into my mind. *You need me.*

I did. I really did.

But it had to be her choice.

Charlotte. I pulled back, her claws raking through my consciousness. *Whatever you choose, I love you.*

And I left her there. Raced back along the dark path to the light, out onto the roof of the building, still holding her against me, her blood on my hands. My vampire had healed her, the bullet hole in her chest sealed over, pink with new skin. She looked so small and vulnerable in only her bra and underwear, both stained with filth and her blood, all trace of the wolf she was gone from her in death.

I waited, held my breath while Gram softly kissed my mind and retreated, her own sorrow powerful, overwhelming. I wiped my tears, fought off the blackness of grief. Charlotte knew I was here, could decide for herself. And whatever her choice, I knew now she made it with my own conscience clear.

I could have forced her to stay. Could have begged, dragged her back with me.

This way, if Charlotte came back to me, it was because she wanted to.

When she drew her first breath, I laughed and cried and hugged her, rocking her again while Quaid sank down beside me, spreading a black robe over her suddenly shivering body. Charlotte's blue eyes opened and met mine, teeth chattering as she reached up with one hand and touched my cheek.

"I love you too," she whispered. "I choose to stay."

Sassafras's purr washed over both of us as he rubbed his furry cheek against hers.

"Coven Leader." Pender's tone was reverential, respectful. I looked up, met his gaze.

He couldn't even give me a second?

"Go." Charlotte coughed softly, sitting up as Quaid leaned in to support her. "I'm fine."

I knew she was. My vampire made sure of that. Still.

Sigh.

I joined Pender as he gestured for me to follow, retracing my steps back to the machine. Sassafras scampered past me, amber flashes of magic shielding him from the sharp shards on the asphalt.

I explained everything while the tall Enforcer leader listened and nodded and shook his head.

"Terrible," he said. "You've saved us all again, haven't you?" Pender's lean face pinched in concern. "You realize you've only put yourself back into the line of fire." So he was just as aware of my impending burning at the stake as Mom, was he? "But I assure you, I will do everything in my power to assure the Council you acted only in our best interest." He straightened, drew a breath, face sad. "I fear there will be many more incidents like this one before we have peace."

If we ever had peace. It was nice to have his support and all, but knowing what I was heading home to face, the fact we hadn't been able to do this quietly left me with a sour taste in my mouth.

Well, if it came down to it, I could always just hide on Demonicon.

Something whispered at my feet. I looked down, surprised to find the orphaned coven magicks, those of the tiny families who'd lost their lives to the Brotherhood clinging to my legs like fearful children.

Pender flinched, tears welling in his eyes, spilling over his cheeks before he brushed them away with a brusque motion.

I almost opened to the magicks. They needed a home, were so lonely, called to me, begged to be allowed in.

Don't be an idiot. Gram's mind slashed across mine. *You want to die, is that it?*

Damn her. *What am I supposed to do, then?*

Someone stepped up beside me. Demetrius Strong's lucidity was long gone, the man I'd met inside the crystal buried under his insanity. But in one trembling hand he held out my crystal, the one I thought I'd lost and as I took it I understood.

With a whispered promise delivered by my family magic, I beckoned the lonely power forward and lured it into the stone, trapping it there.

Now you have proof. Gram's mind eased up, her own sadness making it through. *Well done.*

For an idiot.

Pender left me to talk to three Enforcers who swooped toward us, returning from their pursuit of the Brotherhood. I held out little hope they managed to capture Belaisle, but knowing he was on the run was enough for me. I turned from the crystal machine, the housings and six piles of shards all that remained of the thing, the sound of stone grinding under my feet.

Trill stood behind me, a small smile on her face. Without her glasses, her dark eyes no longer hid behind the glare of the lenses. She looked tired, bone weary, but when she reached out for my hand, her maji power linking with me, I felt her satisfaction.

I agree with Ethpeal, she sent. *Well done. And you're not an idiot.*

Nice to have someone on my side for a change.

Owen slid between us, hugging me before his impossibly blue eyes lit up. "We thought we'd be too late," he said. "Trill tried to reach you when she figured out what you planned."

"How did you do that, by the way?" I draped my arm over Owen's shoulder, raising an eyebrow at Trill.

She blushed and shrugged. "We're still linked together," she said. "Ever since the vampire thing." Oh yeah, that little vampire thing. When I was drained nearly to death and left to float in the veil and she'd saved me, pulled me out of it.

Right.

"You've been spying?" I couldn't bring myself to be irritated or even annoyed. Seemed like the more people who knew what I had going on inside my head, the better these days.

Trill shook her head. "Not me," she said. "Iepa."

For the love of all that was blessed and elemental. That I could get angry about.

Didn't have a chance. Not with tall, blonde, and handsome winking at me again. I thought Quaid had the whole leer thing down to an art. Even my friend Ram back on Demonicon couldn't hold a magic candle to the smarmy smile and eye drooping wink this character threw my way.

Comical, really. Just comical.

Trill rolled her eyes with a heavy sigh and punched him firmly in the stomach. He gasped out a breath of air, doubling over before glaring at her.

"Sydlynn Hayle," she said between clenched teeth, "our brother, Apollo."

Ah. Now it made total sense. "You found him." Was that why he fit between them, between their power?

"Some days I wish we hadn't." She gave him another grumpy look before tossing her hands in the air. "If we didn't need him to channel our two magicks, I'd have kicked his butt to the curb about five seconds after I met him."

Apollo managed to look hurt though Owen laughed.

"Ignore them," he said. "They're always like this."

And I thought my family was quirky.

Trill's eyes went to Pender as he spoke to his Enforcers. "You realize this is far from over."

"Tell me about it." I let my arm drop, sliding the crystal into my pocket, shuddering from the dried blood on my shirt as my shoulder twinged. Not fully healed from being shot yet, it seemed.

"Belaisle only ran because he chose to." Trill crossed her arms over her chest, face serious, pinched and aged well past her years. "He wasn't ready to face us yet. But he will be."

"So you say." Apollo's smarmy smile was back. "We kicked his butt and you know it." He turned sideways, ran his hand through the air. "Like mowing wheat, baby."

I was beginning to understand the tight, hard line between Trill's brows.

Hilarious. And if I had to spend much more time with him, Trill would be down to one brother again.

She didn't bother to even acknowledge Apollo spoke while Owen giggled behind his hand. "I also have no doubt he wasn't lying when he said they have more things in the works."

I thought about Demetrius and Coterie Industries, knowing she was absolutely right.

"They're messing with normals," I said. "And have been for a long time."

Trill looked suddenly nervous. "Syd," she whispered. "Can we really do this?"

I couldn't afford to have doubts. But I knew exactly what she meant. We weren't talking some small time action, here. This mess had grown outside magical purview and into the normal's world.

How would we ever stop them?

"I don't know," I said, leaning forward to hug her. "But we're damned well going to try."

Trill pulled away, nodded. Froze, eyes huge.

Something hit my back, drove me into her. If she hadn't been ready for it, the two of us would have tumbled to the roof. As it was, Trill grunted, body braced against mine, as my magic surged in answer to the assault.

I turned, power raging, to find Mia standing there, her fists in the air, Quaid holding her back as she screamed silently into the night. She didn't make a sound until she drew a breath.

"You did this!" She fought her brother, hissing and snarling and scratching at him while I stood there with my heart wrapped in power, trying not to agree with her.

Failing.

Mia finally stopped fighting, sagging in Quaid's arms before her mouth worked and she spit at my feet.

"You interfered with my coven," she snarled. "And I'll make sure you pay for that interference."

chapter thirty three

I was royally screwed. But I couldn't bring myself to argue, to say anything, standing there with Mia's hate battering at my shields, her weak power not even a threat, though her plan was.

Just my freaking luck.

"I saw it clinging to you!" Mia battered at Quaid with both hands, fury almost enough, despite her weakened state, to break free of her brother's hold. "I know you influenced it, told it what to do. You're working with him, aren't you?" She wailed, a piercing sound before she jerked her body so taut Quaid almost lost control. "He's your pawn. I knew it. I knew it!"

If only she knew how much I wished she was still in control of her family's magic.

"As the Dumont leader," Andre interrupted my grim plan to find a hole to hide in, "I resent such an implication." He turned his nose up at me. "As if anyone from our family would be in thrall to a mere Hayle witch." He sniffed, seriously offended. "Unthinkable."

I'd give him unthinkable. Two minutes alone with him and he'd never think coherently again.

But Andre wasn't done. From the nasty look on his face, it was his turn to pile some kindling on my funeral pyre. "Now that I, the true heir, am in control of our coven, it is my responsibility to bring those who have wronged my coven to justice." Yup, here it came. Arrogant ass. After I saved his family's magic, he was going to stab me in the back while crushing what remained of Mia's spirit.

Classic Dumont tactics. And naturally Pender stood close enough to hear him say it. Charlotte's low, threatening growl told me she'd recovered enough to think she was ready for a fight while Gram's fury vibrated in my head. I faced off with Andre, jaw set, ready for the worst.

Caught the glimmer of regret in his eyes, the clench of his own teeth as he bowed his head to me.

"As Dumont leader," he said as though it pained him, "I find no grievance."

Um, what?

Holy.

Did Andre actually have a conscience?

Amazing.

"The Dumont coven is grateful to the Hayle leader," he said, still with that pained look on his angular face, "for her assistance in returning our family's power to its rightful place at last."

Gram spluttered incoherently in my head as I fought to process what just happened. My stunned silence was broken by Mia's inhuman shriek. She launching herself bodily at him, finding a new target this time, sliding from Quaid's grip at last. I stepped back, keeping my distance, despite my first instinct to make a grab for her.

No way was I getting involved in this, not after my close call, with the Enforcer leader watching all of it. But the spectacle was horrible, heartbreaking to watch as she pummeled Andre's wide chest with her fists, her feeble magic pulling at the core of the Dumont family now firmly in place with her uncle.

He laughed at her. Shoved her so hard she fell to the pebbled asphalt. Quaid's glare of rage did nothing to soften Andre's contempt.

The new leader of the Dumont family bent over weeping Mia. "And now," he said with an edge in the sweet tone of his voice, "it's time to declare you allegiance to your leader." So much terrible joy, too much.

Just too much.

She stared up at him, mute, shattered as he held out his hand, palm up, a ball of lavender magic floating over his skin. Mia flinched from it, shaking her head as he bent low, lips almost next to her ear.

"You'll take it," he said, "and you'll like it."

Filthy, disgusting, core-rotten—

Mia was stronger than I thought, even now. I figured she'd cave. She needed a coven to protect her. That was our way. Without family magic to sustain and shield her, as weak as her own magic was, she wouldn't survive. The terrible loneliness after being part of something so huge would finish her off.

Still. I saw her face firm, her eyes flash fire just before she slapped his hand away.

"Never!" She spit at him much like she'd spit at me, fighting off Quaid as he tried to pull her to her feet. She staggered upright, almost drunk with her rage and loss. "Thief, give back what you stole from me and I'll let you live."

Andre shrugged, turned his back on her. "If you refuse to swear your oath, you are no longer welcome in my family." Better bet he stressed that "my" to the hilt. Just to rub it in a little more.

I really hated his guts, no matter what he did to save mine.

His icy eyes flickered over me, the old Dumont swagger back with a vengeance. "I'll be seeing you, Sydlynn Hayle," he said before looking down his nose at Pender. "I require an escort home so I might reconnect my family power with the rest of my coven." Like Pender and his Enforcers were a taxi service.

Well, they brought him here. So I had to admit it wasn't all that arrogant to need a ride back.

Still.

My stomach did a slow flip over as Pender himself gripped Andre's arm. The Dumont leader's smile never left him as he saluted me before they vanished in an outflux of air and a flash of blue magic.

Mia gaped at the spot where Andre had been, hands rising as though to grasp at his after image. I knew it was none of my business, knew she hated me now, needed someone to blame and I was a convenient target, but I still felt terrible for her.

And was horribly worried we'd made a massive mistake giving Andre control of the Dumont coven.

Not my problem, my new mantra.

Considering the Dumont family track record when it came to my coven, I just hoped "not my problem" was true.

Chapter Thirty Four

"How long exactly were you in possession of the Dumont family magic?" Huan Wong glared at me over her round glasses, lips turned down into a grim half circle, wrinkles pulling at her pale yellow skin.

Oh. My. Swearword.

"For the last time," I said, temper showing as I snapped my response, "I was never, at any time, in control of another family's power."

What, telling them sixteen million times wasn't enough? Sixteen million and one it was.

The entire line of Councilors, Mom included, towered over me in their high and mighty seats while I sat on a low bench in the middle of the chamber, enduring my third round of interrogations since Pender kindly but firmly escorted me to Harvard.

"I'm so sorry," he said. "But I'm under orders."

I could still hear Charlotte's howls as he took me away, leaving her behind. And they hadn't let her or anyone else near me since. Three rounds, three days. Oh, I wasn't a prisoner. They assured me of that the moment I was escorted through the Council main doors and presented like a trussed up turkey at holiday time. Not at all.

They just had some questions.

Yeah.

Right.

"And yet," Huan said, "you claim you did have control during your time inside the crystal column." She glanced to her right where a line of glowing blue writing hovered. She squinted at what she'd written in magic before fixing me with her glare again. "Isn't that true?"

Okay, so I got why Mom allowed this to go on and why she permitted the Santos family to do the poking and prodding. Everyone knew the Dumonts were our enemies. But the Santos family were in close cahoots. So by allowing their Council member to try to tear me a new one showed the Council my mother wasn't acting out of loyalty to her old coven or to her daughter, for that matter.

Logically, it made total sense.

Emotionally, it hurt like hell. And considering the short fuse of my typical temper, three days bordered on a miracle. In fact, she was lucky I hadn't gotten up and walked out already.

Since I wasn't a prisoner or anything.

"Just in case you weren't listening the last twenty times you asked me this question," I said while my vampire's spirit magic whispered patience in counterpoint to my demon raging and throwing fireballs around inside my head, "I never, at any point, had any control over the Dumont family magic. It was in there with me. But I didn't touch it or the other magicks. My focus was destroying the crystal."

"With your sorcery." She tipped her chin down and looked at me without the aid of her glasses. "The very power we're now finding ourselves fighting against."

Was she freaking serious?

Enough.

I was about to rise, and screw them all, when Mom's magic rang like a bell.

"I believe we've heard everything the coven leader has to tell us." She turned to Pender who bowed to her. "Enforcer Leader Tremere, can you attest to the honesty of Coven Leader Hayle's testimony?"

Excuse me?

Was that guilt on his face?

"I can, Council Leader," he said. "As requested, I have been inside her mind the entire time. Everything she's told us is absolutely true as she knows it."

My entire body shuddered, blood rushing to my feet

as I understood. She'd ordered him to spy on me, to invade my mind and I hadn't even known he was there. Even the Council members had the good grace to look uncomfortable though my mother's angry stare never faltered. Huan sat back with her own scowl despite Pender's assurances.

How dared they? How dared she?

"Council will now deliberate." She rose without another word, stalking out of the room, the others following her, whispering to themselves. Erica's unhappiness was clear and I could tell from the way she glared at Mom's back she had no idea what my mother had been up to.

Pender approached slowly, head down, and when he spoke, his voice was apologetic.

"Please forgive me," he said. "I had—"

I surged to my feet, not touching him, rage flaring as the shock of my violation finally hit me. "Orders, Pender? Screw you and your orders. After everything I've done..." I backed away from him as two of his Enforcers rushed forward to defend him, but he waved them off.

"If you will come this way, please," he said, gesturing, not meeting my eyes.

Back to my cell. That wasn't a cell, was it? No, just a nicely appointed suite with a lock on the door and wards on every exit.

I slammed the heavy wooden door in Pender's face

before turning and pressing my back to it. Deep breathing did little to calm me down, my skin prickling with rage. My demon's fury matched mine as she offered a selection of deliciously vicious options for his demise and disposal while Shaylee vented her frustration through a small earthquake shaking my room so hard three pictures fell from the walls and a large carafe of water slid to the tile and shattered.

Let them feel that and wonder.

I understand your anger, my vampire sent. *But we can't afford to be angry yet.*

Yet. *You mean I can freak out and wreck some stuff later?*

She sighed. *Of course*, she said in her long-suffering way. *If you think it will solve anything.*

Nope, not really. But I'd feel better.

You do realize Pender must now know you went to see Ameline. Damn it. Had I gone there, thought about it? I'd been careful to focus on Demetrius so I didn't let anything slip verbally. Used him as my explanation for having the knowledge I did.

If Pender knew, he hadn't said, at least no so far. Which suggested to me he wouldn't.

You're most likely right, she sent, sounding relieved. *I can't believe none of us felt him.*

I reached for Gram, ran into the wall the Council placed around me within moments of arriving three days ago. So no outside support.

I was still a little shocked she hadn't stormed her way into the proceedings and gave Mom what for. For all I knew, she tried and failed.

The worst part of all of it wasn't answering the damned stupid questions over and over again or the glares and judgments from the Council. Or even the way my own mother treated me like a criminal. No, the worst was being cut off from the outside, not knowing what was happening. I could only assume things went on as normal without me because the Council gave no indication there had been more attacks. But a powerful sense of urgency burned inside me, begging me to hurry the hell up and get out there.

I sat on the edge of the sofa and clasped my hands in my lap. They'd taken my crystal away, so no access to my sorcery. Which meant when I tried to reach for Trill I didn't have full access to my creation power. And there was no way I was risking using blood magic directly.

Kerosene with that kindling, Syd?

My attempt to make amends with Mia, there on the rooftop, crashed and burned at least.

"There's always a place for you with the Hayle family." I meant every word, hoped she'd find it in herself to realize it really wasn't my fault. That it was just crappy circumstances compounded by all those years wasted when she was latent.

She turned on me, hissing like a viper.

"You'll pay," she snarled before accosting an Enforcer and making him take her away.

Quaid went with her, eyes locked on mine as they vanished.

It was hard to tell if he blamed me, too.

I then watched, Sassafras coming to my side, Charlotte on the other, as the Enforcers swept up the remains of the machine with their magic and took it away. Demetrius spent the entire time they worked hopping up and down, tearing at his hair. When they vanished, he spun on me, ran to my side.

"Bad, bad," he said.

Not my problem.

Pender appeared shortly after that and everything went to hell.

It wasn't I was surprised they wanted to talk to me or anything. But the way I was treated, that came as a shock. Right from the first moment, when I was cut off, when Pender lifted the crystal from my pocket, when Mom sat back and allowed Huan to take over, to push me and my buttons as far as she could possibly push them while my mother's pet Enforcer violated my mind with his magic, they assured me I wasn't under arrest.

But when I was led here, to this room, and locked inside, I knew it was a lie.

I guessed they didn't dare openly arrest me. Not without proof of some kind. Not considering I'd just saved them again, alerted them to the threat in the first place. And, after my initial testimony and forced discussion of what I was becoming, not one of them was unaware of how much power I now carried.

Which only made it worse, didn't it?

Did it ever.

That lovely first day ended when Mia was led in, her hate firmly in place, a toxic poison leeching from her as she lunged for me, only to be held back by two Enforcers.

Neither of which was Quaid.

"I declare grievance!" She stabbed the air with one finger, stabbed at me with her desperate, impotent rage. "This thief stole my power and gave it to another."

Was it really that easy for them to believe the raving, raging shell standing in front of them over me? Looked like it.

"Explain." Huan leaned in like a hungry shark smelling my blood in the water. Speaking of blood, they hadn't even allowed me to shower or change the first night before they started in on the questioning. I could only imagine I looked about as bad as Mia, covered in my own gore.

Real fear flared in my gut before I pushed it aside.

I had nothing to fear. I could escape this at any moment. Just let the Enforcers try to stop me.

It was my coven I worried about.

Mia rambled, a broken and disjointed story I could hardly follow, part of me feeling very sorry for her, the other part just wanting her to shut the hell up and stop whining about it already.

Probably my demon part. She took the blame, anyway.

Andre's arrival silenced Mia. He swept into the chamber like he was the Council Leader, his two sons at his side. They reeked of magic again, both Jean Marc and Kristophe looking all kinds of smug.

If Andre was the King of Creep, his sons were the Princes of Pompous.

"Might I assure the Council," Andre said with a flowing bow, "none of what the former leader of my coven claims," there was the "my" again, "is true." He turned to me with flourish. "Coven Leader Hayle had nothing to do with the theft of our power but, instead, insured its freedom and return to the family where it belongs."

Even Mom looked startled. "You're speaking in favor of the Hayle coven leader?"

His smile broadened. "I am, indeed, Council Leader," he said. "The Dumont family owes her a great debt of gratitude."

We're even, he sent in a tight line directly to my mind. *Don't ever think otherwise.*

I slashed across the connection between us, cutting

him off. So much for a debt the Dumont family would never be able to repay.

Arrogant ass.

Huan's frown seemed disappointed as she sat back. "Very well, then," she said. "This Council thanks you for your honesty, Coven Leader Dumont."

Andre bowed again before turning away.

"Wait!" Mia's eyes welled, spilled over as she blubbered a moment before pulling herself together enough to speak. "Please, I have to have it back."

Andre's contempt was so thick she could have made a bed out of it.

"Outcast," he said. "Your leadership, or lack thereof, brought our family to its lowest point in our history. It's time for a strong voice and a firm hand. Be grateful the coven doesn't demand your death for our near destruction."

Mia sank to the floor, face in her hands as Andre swept from the room and I cursed him silently.

I couldn't watch as they led Mia out. Carried, actually.

At least I hadn't needed the little technicality Gram and I came up with. Bad enough Mia was so broken. Me rubbing it in she couldn't challenge me because she wasn't a coven leader at the time probably would have just piled on more damage.

The rest of my interrogation went without interruption. Meals, a shower at last, change of clothes.

Sleep. I needed all of those. But after three days of this garbage, I was ready to have it end.

One way or another.

I'd decided early into day two if they chose to charge me, I'd step down as leader of the Hayle coven. For their protection. I knew Gram would want to fight me on that, but I really had no other choice. It would mean she'd need to find someone to take over, a transfer of power and the end of the Hayle name. But it would also mean our family was safe, if under new management.

I could live with that. And would when I ran.

Maybe it would be easier anyway, just to take off. To do what I had to do without the fetters of my kind's society to hold me back. I could join Trill and Owen, even their atrocious brother Apollo, and act behind the scenes. It would mean running for the rest of my life, being a fugitive. Or at least long enough for the witches to forget about me.

Immortality meant I'd outlive them all eventually.

But even though it made perfect sense, I couldn't bring myself to go. Not yet. Not until I knew for sure if it was necessary. Abandoning my family wasn't something I was willing to do lightly.

It burned my ass knowing I'd saved them all again, done everything I could to follow their rules, acting when they wouldn't. Or maybe couldn't. And yet, here I sat, waiting on the judgment of those who had absolutely no clue what they faced.

No pity party. I'd given up on poor me so long ago I barely remembered the girl I was, whining about her life, wanting to be ordinary. This was who Sydlynn Hayle was meant to be. The whole destiny thing? No more fighting it.

No matter what it cost me personally. I'd save them, time and again, for as long as they let me. And even after that. Because that was me.

I felt the seals around the room sigh, heard the door handle turn.

Drew a breath. Stood and squared my shoulders.

My own fate decided, regardless the Council's will, I was ready.

Pender entered, head still down. "It's time," he said.

I strode to his side, pushed past him. "Let's get this over with."

chapter thirty five

Pender let me walk ahead of him, didn't try to touch or escort me. Must have known any attempt would be rejected. It was a short walk, but felt like forever, my feet making dull taps against the old tile floors. University Hall stretched most of the length of Harvard Yard, and the magic floor reserved for the Council ran with long, empty corridors, large windows looking out over the green space. I glanced outside as I walked, gaze traveling over the trees and grass, the sight of late term students going about their lives below stirring my sadness at last.

We'll be fine, my vampire sent, my demon hugging me, Shaylee singing softly as she stroked my mind. The family magic coiled around me, embracing all of us as we passed around the corner and headed for the Council doors.

I know, I sent back, letting them feel how much I loved them. *We're sure, then?* They were all very aware of the choices I'd made, the decisions I'd come to. They'd helped me reach them.

We are, they said in unison while the family power sighed a soft agreement. *We will fight to the last and, if necessary, we will leave our family to protect them.* Even though the family magic inside me tied to my coven hiccupped unhappily, it agreed.

Okay then.

In confident and complete unity of ego, maybe for the first time ever, I strode through the large doors with my head high and my soul at peace. I came to a halt in the middle of the sun-filled room, no longer worried about the future, mine or the coven's. My eyes went to the place I'd sat for so long, noticing they'd removed my chair and left me to stand.

To face their judgment on my feet. No objections.

It was about time.

Huan stared at me over her steepled fingers while the rest of the Council watched me with pinched faces and nervous energy, perhaps more agitated by my calm and confident state than had I shown weakness or fear. "Any last words, Coven Leader Hayle?"

No way was I going to bow and scrape and beg them for mercy just to make them feel better. And while it was ominous, such a choice of phrase, now that she mentioned it, I had a whole hell of a lot to say, thanks.

"I would do it all over again to save you." Flinching,

guilt, one weak, sad smile from Erica answered my words. My voice held steady, my calm wrapped around me like a cloak. "You must know by now the Brotherhood isn't going to just go away because you want them to." Mom didn't move or speak, face a flat mask of anger. "The old ways aren't working anymore. Not while the sorcerers build world-wide conglomerates to control the normals." Frustration simmered as I stared into fearful faces, knowing they would do nothing to act. Mom was right. They would cling to their laws and their secrecy and nothing I said would ever change their minds. Only a radical shift would force them to do anything but hide behind what had been. "If you insist on burying your heads in the sand, the Brotherhood will succeed in their goal to destroy all magic but their own." More fear. Were they listening? It didn't matter. I had my say. Best I could do. "I, for one, won't stand by and allow them to take over without a fight."

Challenge heard. Ignored. One last prod to go.

"And I hope I'm not alone."

Crickets.

Shrug.

So be it.

The brick wall that was the High Council sagged back into their collective seats as I fell silent. Mom traded places with them, finally leaning forward, her angry blue eyes fixed on mine.

"Despite numerous warnings from your Council Leader, you have once again acted outside the laws of your people." Mom's voice carried, deep and full of disappointment.

She had to be kidding me.

"I could say the same of you, Council Leader," I snapped back, temper finally winning. "Not only did you keep vitally important information from this Council and all witches, information that could have meant the loss of witchcraft, you illegally ordered the invasion of a Coven Leader's mind by one of your Enforcers when that coven leader wasn't under arrest." I glared. "By your own words."

The Council didn't move, a frozen tableau of witches staring at Mom, waiting for her response.

As she said they would. Unmoving, unmovable. Frozen in indecision while she took charge.

I just wished she was on the winning side instead of becoming the very heart of what needed changing.

"This Council," she snapped, "has reached a decision on the matter. While we are grateful for your actions on our behalf," yeah, she sounded—and they looked—really grateful, "and are well aware of the consequences of the Brotherhood's activities," I highly doubted that was true, "there have been so many repeated incidents of you and your coven breaking and bending law, we can no longer tolerate your behavior as we once did."

Tolerate my—

Bite me.

"This is your final warning, Leader Hayle." Mom's voice vibrated with her barely contained anger. "This kind of vigilante activity has no place in our society and, from this moment forward, if you step over that line you will be punished to the full extent of our laws." Her knuckles rapped against the table, the sound ringing through the room. "Any and all charges we bring against you shall be retroactive from this point on. We're giving you a pass, but should you push your boundaries again, if you choose to stand on the wrong side of the law, we will bring the full force of that law to bear for every single infraction you've incurred."

Like it mattered. Any one of them, if prosecuted the right way, would mean burning me at the stake. How many times could they crispy critter one prisoner?

Then again, my near-invincibility raised some uncomfortable possibilities.

The idea they could burn me, wait for me to heal and regenerate, only to do it all over again made my blood slow to a cold crawl.

Mom slammed her chair back and stood so abruptly, Huan meeped in fear. "Dismissed."

I stood there and shook as they filed out once more, Mom storming away, explosive anger held in check by the thin thread of a vampire's power as she begged me to keep my temper.

We won, she sent.

For now, I shot back. *But what happens next time? This isn't going to go away. And I have a job to do.*

Not one of my other egos could counter that truth.

And damn me, no matter the consequences, next time I wouldn't hesitate, either.

Still shaking, suffocating in the now dank and oppressive air of the room, I spun and left, head up, the momentary victor in a war I couldn't win.

chapter thirty six

Mom wasn't about to let me off so easy. I'd just stepped outside the front doors of University Hall, preparing to find a quiet place to tear open the veil and just go the hell home when her mind latched onto mine.

Not gently. Not kindly. With force.

My office, she sent. Snarled, really. *Now.*

First impulse? Smartass answer.

Second impulse? Ignore her and get the hell out.

Third impulse won. I trudged across the Yard, the frayed edges of my give a damn hanging around me. All through the last three days I'd been hoping Mom's angry front was just that—a front. A mask to keep the other Council members happy.

But now that I'd felt her mind, heard and touched how real it was, my own anger flared bright and eager for a target.

This really is a bad idea, my vampire sent.

No hitting, Shaylee added.

No mercy, my demon growled.

They were all kinds of helpful.

It was only the layers and layers of shielding I built keeping me from imminent explosion. When I focused on my energy, my temper cooled. I felt Gram battering around the edges, trying to get to me now that I was free, but I wasn't ready to let her in just yet. I knew she had to be worried. I sent her a thin touch of comfort before shutting her out completely just as the elevator doors dinged and whooshed open.

Maurice stood on the other side, his round face pinched in distaste. "Coven Leader," he said as if it hurt him. "This way."

"I know the way," I said. Shoved past him with a wave of magic pushing ahead of me like a battering ram, the shields I'd built forming a shell keeping him from touching me.

Just try to touch me, bugazoid. See how big a smear you make.

Mom's office door gaped open. I stormed through and slammed it behind me, right in Maurice's furious face. Let him be mad. Too freaking bad. I was a coven leader, damn it, and no two-bit bureaucrat with delusions of his own importance would treat me with anything but respect.

Hell yeah.

Mom stood in the window, her back to me, hands clasped behind her. The streaming sunlight cast her in darkness, though her rigidity told me as much as her angry mental connection had.

"Council Leader." No way was she getting more than that from me. Not after what she'd done.

"Coven Leader," she said, voice a deep growl.

"You wanted to see me?" I sank into one of the high-backed chairs in front of her desk, crossing my legs, going for casual. The laws be damned, I hadn't done anything wrong. In fact, I'd done it as much by the book as I could, considering the circumstances. Mia's little hissy fit was just that. And as long as Mom didn't know I'd snuck in to see Ameline, I should be golden.

She didn't turn, didn't move. "I thought we had an agreement." No sadness in her voice, not a touch of motherly concern. Just that hard-edged anger, the coldness of her disappointment.

"We did," I said. "And I followed your rules."

"Until they didn't suit you any longer." She spun then, still in darkness as the light behind her glared around her, but her blue eyes glowed with enough power they were visible. "You were to stay out of it, Syd."

This was bordering on the ridiculous. "Tell me," I said. "What would you have done about the Brotherhood's crystal device if you'd ever found out about it? Which I doubt you would have, considering your track record."

Syd, my vampire whispered. *Careful. Something is wrong here.*

What? I reached for Mom, but she was as sealed off as I was. *Wrong? What do you mean?*

I don't know, she sent, *but your mother feels...*

Dark, my demon growled.

Lost, Shaylee sent.

If they were worried, I needed to be concerned. I reached for Mom again, but with no more luck than the first time.

"This Council," Mom said, "and this office are the last line between witchdom and chaos, Leader Hayle." She was going for the formal, too, following my lead. "And while we're in no way perfect, we have processes and laws for a reason." One of her fists lifted and hit her thigh with a dull thud. "I understand your position. I do. But, Syd, please, you have to listen." She seemed to crumble, body falling forward, shoulders slumping, the statue of anger collapsing into desperate rubble. "They'll kill you next time," she whispered.

I stood and went to Mom, turned her sideways so the sun lit her face at last. Deep lines, lines that weren't there before, creased her face as her cheeks pinched in worry and fear. More silver threaded through her jet hair and her hands, when they gripped mine, were thin and withered. How much pressure was she under? Or, as my egos suspected, was there more going on here?

"Mom," I said, squeezing her hands, "are you okay?"

She shook her head, tried to pull away but I refused to let her go. Tried again to reach her. Finally did when I dropped my own thick shielding. For a moment she felt like nothing to me, gaping emptiness.

There it is, my vampire sent.

But the feeling vanished so quickly, the rush of Mom smothering me only a second later, even my egos seemed confused.

She's hiding something, Shaylee sent. *There's much more to this than she's told you. Than you've uncovered.*

Agreed, my vampire sent.

She'll tell us, my demon snarled.

But standing there in the sunlight with my reduced mother slumped before me, I couldn't bring myself to push her too hard. I let her power hug me, hugged her back physically, the scent of lilacs so powerful it triggered my nausea.

No, not the lilacs themselves, but the rancid edge around them.

What was happening to my mother?

She pulled away, shoulders straightening as she met my eyes, more of the woman I knew and loved in her face than had been since this whole mess began.

"You give me strength, as always." Her fingers

brushed my cheek, a small smile lifting her lips, her whole face.

"Mom," I said. "I know there's something going on with you. Let me help."

She hesitated. And for a heartbeat I was sure she was about to ask. But when she looked away, out the window, her face fell and I knew she would never let me in.

Damn her and her stubbornness. Like I was one to talk.

"There's more," I said. "Things I didn't tell the Council."

Her head whipped around, eyes tightening.

"Trill has information," I said. "About a dark sect of maji—"

Mom's reaction was so powerful I jumped when she jerked away from me, face contorted in a mix of grief and rage.

"Stop!" She turned away, went to her desk, slammed both fists into its surface. "Enough, Syd!"

My anger failed me, weariness taking over. I'd fought so hard for so long, only to meet a wall I couldn't bring down, the wall that was my mother.

"I can't stop," I whispered, voice cracking. "It's my destiny."

She turned toward me, shaking her head, tears tracking down her cheeks. "This is my fault," she said. "Mine. I should have let you go when you wanted to be free."

I gaped at her as my heart broke. "What?"

Mom surged forward, grasped my arms, a hint of madness in her eyes. "If I'd known, Syd, I would have let you go." She sobbed once, released me to cover her face with her hands. "I would never have let this happen to you."

"It wouldn't have mattered." I knew that now, as clearly as I understood who I was becoming. "Mom, I'd be here, like this, regardless. You know that."

She dropped her hands, hugging herself, looking away. "Please tell me you'll obey this time." She met my eyes, that same madness in her. Had I driven her to the brink, the battle between her need to protect me and the magic of the Council tearing her in two?

Ah, my vampire sent. *You might have something there. The Council's power has been indoctrinated for centuries, has it not? And while it doesn't control your mother...*

It lived inside her. Influenced her. Guided her.

Oh, Mom.

"I'm sorry it's come to this," I said. "But we both know there's nothing I can to do change things. I'll keep myself as far under the radar as I can. But I have to stop the Brotherhood, Mom. I don't have a choice, either."

She trembled, arms still squeezing herself tight. "I've done everything I can to protect you," she said. "I have nothing left."

"I know," I said, my sadness for her, for both of us, choking me. Though I stood only two feet from her, it felt like miles. My mother wasn't my mother anymore, couldn't be. Not with the power of the Council position forcing her to be Leader first.

And though I hated what I had to do to her, destiny called me. And I knew better than to ignore it.

"I wish things were different." I hugged her again, gently, feeling how frail she'd become, how thin. She didn't embrace me, though she laid her cheek against mine, her skin cold and clammy. "We should be on the same side. But I know you have other powers to answer to, Mom. So do I." I leaned away. "You're my mother. I love you no matter what. Whether we end up on opposite sides, whether the power you carry forces you to act against me." She shuddered, tears trickling down her cheeks. "I get it, and I understand now." She sobbed once, softly, head bowing. "But, Mom, for the love of the elements, keep your eyes open and stop holding things back from the rest of the Council."

She swiped at her nose with the sleeve of her blouse. Bobbed a nod.

"Maybe that way we can keep me out of prison." It came out in a half joke, but it really wasn't funny.

I kissed her softly, sent her love before turning and leaving her there, struggling with her loyalty to me and her ties to the Council power. When I took one last look back, she was still there, trembling and hugging herself, so close to broken I wanted to rush back inside and save her.

Couldn't. I could barely save myself these days. And despite knowing now I couldn't count on Mom any more, what I told her was the complete truth.

I had to bring the Brotherhood down, would do anything, no matter what it took.

The image of Ameline in her cell, smiling at me, triggered one exception.

Almost anything.

chapter thirty seven

Gram's arms squeezed me tight as I stepped through the veil and into the edge of the park. She must have felt me coming despite my attempts to keep her out.

"Girl," she whispered in my ear. "I worried."

"Me too," I whispered back. "Still am."

Gram leaned away, lower lip quivering a moment before she shook her head, frown pinching her brow. "She wouldn't let me near you," Gram said. We both knew who "she" was. And the way Gram said it sounded like Mom was in very hot water.

"There's more to it than we thought." I shared the understanding with her, the way Mom felt and Gram hissed, one hand covering her mouth.

"Miriam," she whispered. "Damn her. She could have told us."

Instead of trying to do it all herself? Not a Hayle trait

or anything.

"Her hands are tied," I said as I crossed into the yard, the wards welcoming me home. Gram followed, one hand sliding into mine as the grass swished under her fuzzy socks. I looked up to find Charlotte standing in the middle of the green space, watching me.

Not freaking out I'd been gone so long.

I wasn't sure if that was a good sign or not.

My bodywere shuddered as I came to a halt in front of her, the wolf flickering in her eyes before she settled into her usual stoic stare.

"Hi." I hugged her, not knowing how she'd receive it. I'd left her for dead, no matter how I looked at it, twisted it. She'd hovered on the edge of leaving me forever and I'd left her to choose.

Charlotte's arms wound around me, pulled me tight as she whispered something in her mother tongue. I didn't catch the words themselves, but the feeling of her was as familiar as it could get.

"I love you, too," I whispered back.

She smiled at me as we released each other, blinking tears from her blue eyes. It always struck me so odd how young she looked when she smiled, just a girl like me, with too much weight on her shoulders.

I had to find ways to make her smile more often.

Charlotte's hand released me, a little frown of sadness flashing as her smile disappeared. But she didn't comment and though I had a million questions to ask her, and a whole heap of gratitude to share, I didn't get the chance.

The back door flew open and Shenka ran out, taking her turn to hug me just as Sassafras's silver body streaked toward me. I lifted him into my arms once Shenka let me go, feeling his purr rumble through my whole body.

My family. Who loved me.

They were worth all of it.

Even Demetrius's face, peeking out the door, big blue eyes wide, a foolish grin on his cherub face, filled me with joy.

"I'm making pancakes," Gram said, linking arms with me.

"At five in the afternoon." Of course she was.

I let the door squeak shut behind me, closing out the rest of the world.

Trouble could wait while I ate breakfast for dinner with the ones I loved.

Thud. Thud.

My fists pounded at the heavy bag in the quiet gym, body tingling with the need to just beat the crap out of someone.

Some*thing* would have to do.

The last few hours hadn't gone exactly as I planned.

I'd had about ten minutes of stogging sweet pancakes into my face before someone knocked on the front door.

I could feel Liam before it even opened, felt a swell of gratitude he'd come to see me, rushed from my chair to hug him.

Almost took out Sonja who slid in beside him with her false smile on her face.

"Oh, Syd," she gushed as Liam's face tightened, "we were so worried about you, dear."

I. Just. Bet.

All of my warmth and welcome ran out of me like she'd punctured my soul. "Thanks," I said as I turned my back on them. Liam's hand settled on my arm, tried to spin me around, but honestly? I'd had it.

I didn't just spend three freaking days defending my freaking right to live after saving the freaking witching world just to have Liam's freaking annoying-ass mother scrape the peeling from my last nerve.

Shenka hustled them out, the sound of her soothing voice doing nothing for the rising irritation taking over. I slammed out of the kitchen and to the back door, letting the screen hit with more force than necessary.

Just as Quaid's power engulfed me.

He stood there, jeaned and t-shirted, chocolate eyes full of need, dark hair begging for my fingers to wind through, lips parted.

Lips I wanted to kiss, bite, crush with my own.

Damn them both, these men in my life. Anger flashed inside me, washed over onto Quaid who took a step back, hands up.

"I'm not him," he said in his deep, velvet voice.

"You're not mine, either," I said. "And you never will be."

Yeah, it was that kind of talk.

Quaid dropped his hands, face settling into calm. If I'd hoped to trigger a fight—okay, I did, so sue me, a good fight would have been perfect right about then—he wasn't taking me up on my attempt.

"I just wanted to make sure you were okay." He stuck his hands into the back pockets of his jeans. "And to tell you how amazing you are."

Not in the mood for flattery.

But he could keep going. Just in case I changed my mind.

"I'm sorry about Mia." Quaid's face fell at last. "She's totally broken now, Syd."

My temper cooled and I nodded. "I figured. I'm sorry, too."

Quaid shrugged, bitterness flashing in his eyes. "Our parents never gave us a chance," he said. "Our whole family was against us. I guess it's just one of those things."

His words made me flinch. I had the most amazing family and I knew it now. I would have argued that point once, but not anymore. I knew how lucky I was. How damaged Quaid and his sister were thanks to Odette and

Claire and the mess their coven made of their young lives.

Quaid closed the distance between us, arms going around me. Not with heat or passion. With comfort, a safe place to harbor and I took it. Pressed my cheek against his chest, listened to his heartbeat, felt my body temperature warm to match his.

We'd severed our private connection over a year ago, when in a fit of rage I cut him off. When I thought he'd abandoned me. I still missed it, wished I could have it back, as selfish as that connection was.

Because he couldn't be mine.

That's why I was so shocked to feel it wake. Not broken, not severed after all. Just silenced.

Until now.

Quaid's arms tightened and I knew he felt it too. I didn't fight it, let it rise, shake, grow until it was as if it had never been gone. He trembled where he stood, and I know I shook too, tears rising at the joy of having him back again.

"Syd," he whispered. "I—"

He jerked free of me, spinning sideways, the sound of flesh hitting flesh loud in the back yard as Liam, face a mask of rage, threw a punch taking Quaid full in the jaw. I stared, in so much shock I couldn't react, watched Quaid stagger back, hand going to his face, heard the deep, rumbling growl come from his chest as he lunged forward.

Toward Liam.

Who snarled back.

They froze within inches of each other, Quaid's dark bulk against Liam's tall brightness.

"You're lucky I don't kill you for that, fairy boy," Quaid said in a voice like gravel.

"Don't touch her," Liam rumbled back, his own deep tone full of fury. "Don't ever touch her again."

Um, excuse me?

"I thought we were done with this." My cold rage turned them both to face me, Quaid sullen, Liam full of righteousness. "Neither of you own me. Or have any right to fight over me."

Liam's face crumpled, his hurt clear as he held out his hand, blood dripping from his knuckles. "You chose me," he said.

"I did," I snapped, "but I reserve the right to change my damned mind. And guess what?" I slashed my own hand through the air, letting a cascade of multi-colored sparks fall from the air. "You just blew it."

Quaid's anger turned to a smirk.

Wrong choice.

"You can both take yourselves and just go to hell." I turned my back on them, closing off the connection to Quaid no matter how much my demon begged, leaving them to beat the crap out of each other if that was what they really wanted.

None of my damned business.

I couldn't stay in the house, not now. Not while Gram watched me with slitted eyes and Shenka tiptoed around me.

I was in no mood for sympathy or a lecture, thanks.

My gym stuff sat near the front door. Begging me to get the hell out. So I did.

And ten minutes later, I hit the heavy bag with all the pent-up rage I'd kept inside me for days and days. For what felt like forever.

A shoulder pressed to the other side, sea-green eyes watching me quietly, without question. I stopped punching, panting to catch some air, dropping my hands to my sides as Sage dug in.

"You're a little off tonight," he said. "Out of focus. Won't do you any good in a fight. Now, jab, jab, uppercut, roundhouse. Hit it like you mean it."

I did. Over and over again, doing as he told me, losing myself, my frustration, my fears in the rhythm of the bag, my body, fists, feet.

"Good." Sage's voice broke the spell, his grin lopsided and delicious.

Damn it. Stop that.

"Thought you quit on me," he said as I sank to the mat to catch my breath. "Didn't seem like you."

"Just had some family stuff to take care of." I rested my forehead on my knees.

"Left your bodyguard home this time." He sat beside me while I looked up, startled.

Looked for Charlotte. Who wasn't there.

So. Weird. Charlotte was always there.

Sage bumped my shoulder with his. "Not to butt in or anything," he said. "But you look like you could use a night off."

I met his eyes, the steady seriousness tempered by a kind heart and felt myself let go at last.

"You know what?" I stood up and offered him my gloved hand. He took it with a grin. "That sounds like a fantastic idea."

And to hell with the rest of it.

chapcer chircy eighc

I was positive my life was meant to be insane at the best of times.

And I guess I was okay with that.

Demetrius's usual disappearing act didn't happen this time around. In fact, he happily ensconced himself in the basement, hugging me with tears in his eyes when I helped him set up a little space for himself with a "real bed" and "clothes of his own".

One more heartache in a long list of them. But at least he seemed content to stay and I wasn't about to kick him out.

Not when I knew I'd been needing him again, sooner rather than later. In fact, despite Demetrius's new digs, he was rarely home, more than eager to seek out the Brotherhood for me. And while I now worried about him, I knew I didn't need to. Demetrius might have reminded me of a scuttling cockroach lurking in the dark, but it was that very trait that kept him safe for so long.

His poking about also meant I kept my nose clean. For now.

I'd take it.

My internet searches of the Brotherhood's corporation turned up frightening results. One of the largest in the world, Coterie Industries controlled massive amounts of land, businesses and government contracts, spreading out like a sickness from the central core. My disgust was equal to my grudging admiration. They'd done what no magical race had ever accomplished. Fit in. More than that. They'd taken over.

It made me wonder if I needed to start finding some of my own allies in the normal world, despite the laws against it.

My burning pyre was calling again.

Tallah finally reached us, by phone of all things, furious. She gave me hell for putting Shenka in danger before thanking me for saving all of our asses again. The weird conversation ended with Shenka fighting for the handset with a pissed-off expression on her face while Tallah informed me if I got her sister arrested she'd kill me personally.

I left the two Hensley sisters to yell at each other and walked away.

Family. Sheesh.

Quaid stayed in touch, my only real line to what was happening in the witch arena since no one else would really talk to me. We were careful not to talk about his fight with Liam or the fact we were linked to each other again. All business, he sadly informed me Mia was trying to form her own coven after her last appeal to the Council failed. He didn't have to tell me what I already knew. She wasn't strong enough to lead when she had all the power of the Dumonts at her disposal. And now? In her weak state, her attempt would only end in disaster.

She managed to gather a few witches, Quaid told me, though they were only with her because they had nowhere else to go. Andre's first act as leader when he arrived home was to cull the herd. It surprised me, considering how many members the family lost in the Brotherhood's assault, their numbers already down to a third of their original strength. But according to Quaid, Andre was making it very clear if the witches in his coven couldn't pull their own weight, they were on their own.

Harsh and arrogant and just cruel. Andre's iron fist knew no mercy, it seemed. And, it appeared he had no intention of allowing his family to fall back into female hands. Quaid's disgust at Andre's choice of Jean Marc as his second resonated with me.

The Dumont family was in for a very hard time. I wondered what the rest of the covens, all matriarchal, were thinking about this male takeover of what was traditionally a woman's position.

They had to be nervous. I know I was, but not for the obvious reason. Despite the fact he kept his promise, Andre Dumont was not to be trusted and I had no doubt his mother's aspirations to gather more power were inbred into Odette's son.

Time would tell. Not my problem, right?

Let Mom deal with it.

Pender finally returned my crystal. The moment it touched my hand I realized my mistake—the other coven's magicks still resided inside it. I could feel the power settling in to their new home and, though I felt terrible for the oversight, there was no way I was telling the Council now.

No way.

So odd Pender hadn't said a word. He'd seen me take the magicks on, hadn't he? Maybe I had an ally I wasn't expecting, if one who simply protected me by omission.

Gram, Shenka and Sass all agreed I should keep my mouth shut and, when I thought about it, I grumbled to myself I should have let the crystal absorb the Dumont power, too, before anyone knew it was there. There would be no proof it hadn't been destroyed by the Brotherhood. And maybe it would have meant the end of a truly evil coven.

Again, not my problem. What was this habit I had of poking my nose in?

Varity Rhodes was making herself at home, coming to visit frequently. I loved to sit and listen to her and Gram talk, the pair of them cackling like old hens, though when I asked for stories of their days together as Enforcers, neither of them would tell me a thing.

Spoilsports.

My birthday came and went, the Beltane celebration embraced by the family who rallied to me as they had never done before. They were well aware of how close they came to losing their leader and, from the support I felt as I lit the Beltane fire, the outswell of love they practically smothered me with, I knew they were behind me no matter what happened.

Which only firmed my resolve to leave them if it came to my own imminent destruction. I'd save them if it killed me.

My shoulder healed from the bullet wound, but I still felt twinges now and then, mostly when I sparred with Sage. Now more than ever I knew I had to improve my fighting skills. There might come a time I couldn't use magic to defend myself. It surprised me when Charlotte asked if she could join me, no longer hanging back. Sage welcomed her, though I could tell from the widening of his eyes when she threw her first punch she'd impressed him.

Impressed the hell out of me. Though I was sure she didn't mean to tear the heavy bag from the ceiling.

Oops.

It was nice to go out with Sage from time to time, have a burger, laugh, be normal. He didn't push me despite the fact we both felt an attraction. I'd been down this road too many times and, in all honesty, I needed a friend more than anything. He seemed okay with our arrangement and I found myself turning to him more often than I did to Liam or Quaid when I just wanted to talk.

Felt good to be ordinary now and then.

As for Charlotte, she seemed perfectly fine. On the outside. The first night when I returned home from my date with Sage, she'd firmly and angrily informed me if I left her behind like that again, she'd chain me to my bed and never let me leave the house.

Odd, considering she should have been able to just track me down thanks to the link between us. Still, I took the threat seriously, apologized enough times she finally cooled off and promised myself I'd not give her reason to regret her choice to come back.

I knew her well enough to catch the moments of panic crossing her face when I turned to leave a room without her. Her own wound healed as though she'd never been shot, but when I asked her how she was doing, she ignored my question. She followed me even more closely than usual, reaching for me occasionally as if to reassure herself I was there. She was freaking me out a little, but that was Charlotte.

She'd taken a bullet for me. Died and come back for me.

I was okay with cutting her some creepy slack.

Trill checked in regularly, even sending me a card with a sweet note inside: *Happy birthday to the sister I never had.* It made me teary. And think of Meems.

I really needed to talk to my sister.

My questions about the dark maji went unanswered, though. Trill finally asked me to leave them to her and I backed off. Not like I didn't have my own crap to deal with. I had to start trusting the people around me to do their jobs while I did mine.

The reconnect of my power to Quaid's made me uncomfortable at times, though I took great comfort from his magical presence. Why was it every time I tried to cut him loose I ended up reeling him back in? It wasn't fair to either of us.

Or to Liam. I knew he was doing his best with Sonja, but I was so done tolerating the woman. He came crawling, begging me to forgive him. I agreed, though I told him friendship was all I could handle right now, after all. Knew I broke his heart.

I'm sure Sonja was thrilled. Though despite his assurances to the contrary, she still remained a pain in my backside. With the craziness of my life and constant threats looming on the horizon, the last thing I wanted was to deal with his overbearing mother.

Single again. Yup yup.

Speaking of mothers... I tried several times to reach out to Mom, knowing now what was going on with her and wanting to support her if I could. But she wouldn't let me in, kept a cold front between us and I finally stopped trying. Maybe if I distanced myself from her, she'd be able to find her own balance. Not be forced to fight against the power she wielded. With time, with a little space, Mom might get a chance to wrangle the Council power under her control and come to the dark side.

No more meddling. I just made things worse.

My maji power was stronger than ever, the crystal helping a great deal when I focused on my exercises. I felt like I was so close to some kind of breakthrough, but still had the impression I was missing something. My goal was simple—to be able to access my maji abilities whether I was in trouble or not. I was tired of only being able to connect when my life—or the lives of those I cared about—were in danger. Mom tried to tell me years ago, how important it was to be in control, to act and not react.

She was right about that, at least.

It was time to visit the maji chamber again, and soon. To track down Iepa if I could, ask her about Ameline. Only trouble was, when I reached out to talk to Sebastian, he didn't respond. In fact, none of the vampires did. My invitation to my birthday sent to Uncle Frank and Sunny went unanswered and all attempts I made to reach Sebastian went cold.

That just wouldn't fly.

Above all else, I hated being ignored.

Like what you read? Find out more at
pattilarsen.com

Here's a look at the first chapter of
Book Sixteen of the Hayle Coven Novels

The Undying

chapter one

The sound of giggling witches filled my back yard. Giggling. And not young witches, either. The Lawrence twins twittered beside Talee Happern while Mary Gripper gossiped over her baby son, Alex, and how he was keeping her awake.

I did my best to plaster on a smile, hoping it didn't look like a grimace, wishing I was back at the gym. I'd doubled my efforts since the run-in with the Brotherhood, the twinge in my shoulder where Liander Belaisle shot me a reminder of just how serious things had become.

Deadly serious. Like almost losing Charlotte serious. The weregirl kept her distance, watching from outside the party, eyes locked on me at all times. And though she was as protective as ever—worse, sometimes, it seemed—I sensed something was wrong with her. The way she flinched when I asked her a question or the way her blue eyes would fill with almost desperate anxiety.

She'd been shot herself, at the doorway to death, only the wolf inside her clinging to life, the ego of her wereside trying to hold her back. And I'd let her go, to choose life or death despite knowing I could have brought her back, maybe made things easier for her.

I tried not to feel guilty about it as I smiled wider, a glass of punch clutched in my hand as I made my way through the group of laughing women. She'd come back, by choice, my Charlotte. But she hadn't been the same since.

Near death would do that to a body, I guess.

Everyone I passed smiled at me, though no one tried to stop me, thank the elements. It freaked me out, to be honest, the way they looked at me. I tried to convince myself it wasn't awe, wonder on their faces.

A little full of ourselves these days. Gram's mental voice cackled in my head. I was about to protest when she slapped my mind with her magic. *You should be. You deserve it. As long as you don't let it screw you up when it counts.*

I glared at her over a gaggle of gray haired witches. Gram just wiggled her fingers at me in a wave and flashed her teeth.

So unhelpful.

I could have been at the gym. Working out. With Sage. Okay, so being with Sage was higher on my to-do list than working out. Though learning to fight was a close second.

I think I impressed him, too, when I came back from my brush with the Council with a new attitude.

"Kick my ass," I told him. "I need to learn how to kick yours."

Sage just nodded, smiled. And gave me the worst beating of my life. Not hard enough to leave bruises. Well, not many. But embarrassing enough I was ready to crawl in a hole and never come out.

By the time he crouched over my prone, groaning body lying on the mat, I was ready to quit.

"How was that?" Sage's smile was the same as ever, pulling against his lips, bit of scruff on his wide jaw darkening at the cleft in his chin while his sea-green eyes laughed at me.

Laughed. At. Me.

Oh *hell* no.

I punched him right in that beautiful nose of his, sending him back onto his own butt with a shocked look on his face.

Didn't last long. The smile came back ten times as bright.

"You'll do," he said.

"I'm done." I collapsed, all out of everything.

Sage stretched out next to me, waist dipping as he rolled on his side, big shoulders looming over me, cheek in his hand. "You didn't give up," he said softly. "You were down, I came in to gloat and you took your shot."

Guilt. Gulp. "Are you okay?"

He touched his nose with his glove and shrugged. "You hit like a girl." Winked.

Laughing hurt. But he was right.

A Hayle family trait. No matter how far we fell, we saved up enough strength to take the last hit.

Things progressed much better from there, though I still lost every bout. I could feel myself growing stronger, though as I side-stepped two laughing girls I felt a jab in my obliques from a blow Sage landed earlier. One of these days I'd win.

Couldn't wait.

At least getting my butt thrashed by a deliciously handsome and very sweet guy almost every day helped me to forget my boy troubles somewhat. Sage was a casual relationship, could never go beyond that and I knew it. Without magic, not even latent, all Sage and I could ever really be were friends. And I was okay with that.

Friends I could handle. Boyfriends? Yeah, not so much.

Sashenka Hensley waved from the refreshment table, dark skin glowing in the light of the setting sun. This garden party was her idea. Naturally. As my second, she took her new role very seriously, doing everything she could to bring the family closer together. They adored her completely, down to the last member. While they looked at me like I might suddenly explode all over them, they turned to Shenka as though they could tell her anything.

The stress of the Brotherhood attack on the Dumonts this past spring took a toll on all witches, but our coven was stronger and more confident than ever, mostly thanks to Shenka. I knew word got around to everyone about my part in the mess, overheard family members talking about it from time to time.

It made me uncomfortable, the way they talked about me, as bad as their awed staring. Like I was special. Unreachable. Undefeatable. I just hoped their faith in me wasn't unfounded. Even though I'd been able to muddle through so far, I had no doubt the worst was yet to come.

So weird, really, considering just a few short years ago they all accused me of being the downfall of the Hayle family. Of putting our coven at risk for no reason. And while I totally understood their previous opinions, since I'd been a bit of a brat and fought my destiny, this new hero worship they threw at me every time I came near felt worse.

I struggled with feeling alone for a long time, ever since I was young. I wasn't, not really. Would never be, not with three hitchhiking souls in my head. But the more the coven put me on their little magic pedestal, the more nervous I became.

I never wanted to let them down.

Smile. Shenka's lips widened at me, dark eyes reflecting the sunset. *You look like you're going to your own funeral*.

Oops. Guess mine slipped. I tried again only to have Shenka laugh in my head.

Okay, she sent, *no smiling. Unless someone is torturing you with magic to put that expression on your face*.

No, I sent back, a real smile rising, *but I'm being tortured, all right*.

She laughed in my head even as she laughed out loud to something one of the ladies said to her. *We're almost done*, she sent. *Thanks for being a good sport*.

Silly, I sent. *This was a great idea. Sigh. I just wish I was as good at it as you are*.

You have more important things to worry about. Shenka met my eyes. *Let me take care of the family*.

Now you know why it's so important to have a second. Gram's mind touched us both. *One you can trust. And why I pushed your ass to find one*.

Bossy. *Yeah, yeah*, I sent. I paused to steady Tara, the demon daughter of Talee who hugged me quickly after almost falling as she fled from some of the other girls in a game of tag before tearing off with peals of laughter. *You were right. You always are. Happy?*

Very. I looked up and into Gram's face. She'd approached without me noticing, standing in my space, nose almost touching mine. *Very, girl. Because I know now, no matter what, you have everything you need.*

I hugged her while she grunted before hugging me back. "Smartass grandmother," I whispered.

She kissed my cheek with a wet smack before twisting out of my grip and flouncing off with her fuzzy socked feet dancing over the grass.

Despite her happy air, why did those words feel ominous?

About the Author

Everything you need to know about me is in this one statement: I've wanted to be a writer since I was a little girl, and now I'm doing it. How cool is that, being able to follow your dream and make it reality? I've tried everything from university to college, graduating the second with a journalism diploma (I sucked at telling real stories), am part of an all-girl improv troupe (if you've never tried it, I highly recommend making things up as you go along as often as possible). I've even been in a Celtic girl band (some of our stuff is on YouTube!) and was an independent film maker. My life has been one creative thing after another—all leading me here, to writing books for a living.

Now with multiple series in happy publication, I live on beautiful and magical Prince Edward Island (I know you've heard of Anne of Green Gables) with my very patient husband and multitude of pets.

I love-love-love hearing from you! You can reach me (and I promise I'll message back) at patti@pattilarsen.com. And if you're eager for your next dose of Patti Larsen books (usually about one release a month) come join my mailing list! All the best up and coming, giveaways, contests and, of course, my observations on the world (aren't you just dying to know what I think about everything?) all in one place: http://smarturl.it/PattiLarsenEmail.

Last—but not least!—I hope you enjoyed what you read! Your happiness is my happiness. And I'd love to hear just what you thought. A review where you found this book would mean the world to me—reviews feed writers more than you will ever know. So, loved it (or not so much), **your honest review would make my day**. Thank you!

www.ingramcontent.com/pod-product-compliance
Lightning Source LLC
Chambersburg PA
CBHW060531180626
46817CB00002B/513